ISBN 978-99987-821-0-5 (ebook)

ISBN 978-99987-821-1-2 (paperback)

ISBN 978-99987-821-2-9 (hardback)

First edition April 2025

Dedication

To my mom, my dad, and the magical night that created me
by mistake.
To my perfectly imperfect siblings.
To everybody who cares… or not.

Fondly Yours,
Lady Seely Clown

Overrated – I said it first.

DISCLAIMER

H ERE WE ARE... TREADING LIGHTLY.

Too bad – this is not a book, a life coaching guide, or a spicy romance novel.

Relax, SMILE! It's just my first attempt at writing.

Some might say I should have not tried – I won't cross swords with them.

Who am I?

I'm a non-certified comedian who uses humor and parody to cope.

Beautiful Earthlings may cringe at most of my jokes and my poetry experiment.

I will either be everyone's cup of tea or no one's.

Originally only for me, myself, and I, this manuscript just turned into a lifesaving endeavour.

Still, you won't get 13 shades of gray, 13 lessons to better your life, 13 lessons to find the perfect match, 13 lessons to cure your self-diagnosed ADHD, or 13 lessons to understand geopolitics, economy, and culture. It's just a simple, silly, cozy fiction/fantasy written by a pantser.

As you can see, I'm also a ditherer who can't even decide if this should be considered fiction or fantasy, a journal or a diary. After feeling stuck in that chicken-and-egg situation, I established it's not that deep. Call it how you want to; it doesn't matter, as No One will read this the same way.

The first goal is for you to remain the exact same person before and after reading this.

Why? I firmly believe that I don't need to change, and I'm pretty sure I'm not that special, so if I don't need to, you don't either.

No opinion or taste should be altered.

Life changes, but people rarely do, and they'll die happily ever after. It's true. Look at me – I just wish to remain a nobody forever. I'm okay.

The second goal is for us to find a smile – including mine. If it didn't work yet at line 3 of this disclaimer, let's try and find one together in this fictional satire. So, if your eyes cross its edge on a bad day, you'll remember something that will make you smile and hopefully shift your mood. Easily amused folks like me can even reach a good laugh, but that will be a bonus. Considering the world we live in, I figured a smile (or a laugh) on demand is something we all need.

Just so we can enjoy this without any issue, it's important for you to know that it's fiction, the product of my unlimited imagination, and "any resemblance to anything, like anything, actual places, events, incidents, entities, fictional characters, real persons, living or dead, is purely coincidental."

To delusional people who might be tempted to make it about themselves, please restrain yourselves. It's just synchronicity. But if your delusional self can't help it, please ask me directly. I already have the answer: "No, it's not about *you*; yes, you are extremely delusional."

To my dear imaginary readers, please don't bring my fantasies into a real world that is already crazy enough.

But if you need to talk, you'll find me.

If not, I hope I'll find *you*, or maybe my algorithm will.

To my dear curious friends, you might be here because of clickbait or trendbait.

Bad news: the topic that interests you may only cover 0.001% of this typescript.

Good news: you can make it the main subject at the end. Open an Autopilot-free word processor file, take a sheet of paper at home, or buy a notebook and start writing.

Trigger warning: brace for impact!

I don't think it's suitable for children under thirteen. If you're a minor, please ask your parents' opinion before reading this and try to respect it for once. Keep your distance from addictions and sorrow.

Special mention to sensitive people: please avoid going further; I promise it's not worth it. I'll try to do the good news/bad news thing. But sometimes bad news is bad news; suck it up please.

If you struggle in any way, please seek real-life help, call hotlines, and reach out to anyone available.

It started as a fantasy diary, so if you already suffer from emotional dumping in real life, you better close this right now.

If truth be told, I still tend to avoid speaking about myself. Undeniably, I'd rather take part in small talk and discuss fun facts than dig deep into my feelings. You should then look at the remaining content as a fantasy newspaper without the proper editing and formatting, written by a wannabe-neutral and opinionless journalist... wannabe.

Believe me, I always try not to take sides if I'm not concerned, even in fantasy.

I want to keep it as light as possible, and the colloquial style should be enough to convey it's not that serious. It might bother conventional bibliophiles, but I use it on purpose because I don't want to exclude anyone from the smile hunt. Everybody's included! There are only two rules: respect and fun.

To those who were born to argue and defend, please don't jump to conclusions; everything from now on is alleged.

To those who fancy projection, please bear in mind that nothing should be considered a criticism of any fictional character; it's all love in Lady Seely Clown's fantasy world.

Please also note that this palimpsest can be filled with fictional inconsistencies and will feel rushed as it's written on short notice (fingers crossed for 13 days or a fortnight) because I did not choose the deadline. I also procrastinated and lacked inspiration. But I still want to say that I achieved something in XX24.

Next year, when asked what's new in my life, I'll proudly say: "I'm an ARTIST."

So, don't be too shocked if you see a grammar or vocabulary mistake; it's part of the artistry as I'm not a native English speaker, but I decided to write in English for some mystical reason. I also love making up words and tongues, which is still part of the artistry.

Additionally, my writing is strictly organic, exempt from digital brains, which explains its flaws. But at least it's mine. I wouldn't change that for anything in the world. That's the beauty of it.

If you're intolerant of first-person narrative, time travel, tense drift, and point-of-view switches that reflect my imaginary multiple personality disorder, make sure you have your ExquiPen at close range.

Don't mind typos, unplugged plot holes, blank spaces, paragraph misuse and endless chapters; this is ART.

The more you find, the closest you get to decipher the code that opens the Treasured Safe.

The chaotic punctuation is also intentional.

Please don't mention... ..these or... .that in the artistic review.

It's ART!

Other artistic decisions: I won't properly introduce or describe all fictional characters and places so that you can better use the power of your mind and enjoy this conceptual writing project.

It is a game, a hunt, that people who are allergic to fun and addicted to boredom should avoid playing.

What are we looking for?

I don't know yet.

I almost forgot to mention that I have the bad habit of losing my train of thought, so hang in there, please.

We might lose the thread, but we'll get somewhere.

Where?

I don't know yet.

PROLOGUE

H ELLO, BEAUTIFUL EARTHLING.

Nice to meet You – inhabitant of my favorite planet in the Solar System.

My name is Seely Clover – formally known as Lady Seely Clover, and I live on Planet X.

The story of my honorary title, *suo jure*, deserves a book of its own. In the meantime, you can call me however you wish – it doesn't matter.

You are most welcome to my humble abode on Polite Village's Camelia Street, in a coastal hidden gem of Great Banter Land (+; +), the cradle of Grits – subjects of The Royal Unicorn family.

Do not bother any real-life Earthling named Seely Clover, if any; they have nothing to do with this.

To be 100 percent sure you don't, I've decided to use my childhood nickname, Lady Seely Clown.

My parents say I've always been a silly, clever girl.

Who am I to tell them what they should think about their child? Especially considering I am a husbandless, childless, and even catless lady who seems unable to keep anything besides her depressing job. If you ask, I agree with silly, but I would never dare to call myself clever. None of my employers would either. I've always been a little pawn in their chessboard. That's one of the reasons why we are here today. After years of trying to fit in a world that doesn't want me, I decided to take my fantasy and destiny into my own hands.

Look what they're making me do...

Everyone has a moment in their life when they have a clear vision of what the future holds for them. It can happen randomly, one day in kindergarten, on high school graduation day, or on a bad day at work. It can happen several times (every end-of-year for me) or just once, watching *The Fate You Can't Escape*, an interesting imaginary movie being played on TV starring... You.

Each step you took, each path you followed, every decision you made, and every decision that was made for you inevitably led to where you are and where you're heading.

Then, you start imagining the sequels based on the characters from the latter:

- *The CEOs* is a biopic-style film about the luckiest people who have it all. They are overprotected by bodyguards, fly private, and throw slumber parties on yachts, but most importantly, they have access to the best healthcare in the world. Life is good and will always be – until the world ends! They made it; be happy for them, and don't be toxic. Instead, find a craft, perfect it, work, beach!

- *The Unfortunate Bunch* is a comedy-drama film about those who are content to be alive and feeling this moment. I relish the scene when they're driving on a mountain road with heavy snow and fog but no tire chains because it was supposed to be sunny. They are the chosen ones who got the hardships and tribulations pack. Surprisingly, even underappreciated, they still manage to find this life beautiful. They still trust the process. Standing ovation, ladies and gentlemen! And... the pronouns. (*Robean's voice*)

- *In Between Both* is an action film about mountain climbers with strength, tools, and often the help of amazing sherpas. We know they'll reach the top of the summit; nothing can hold them down; they're fighters. They know the risks, and they are up for the challenge.

- *The Beauty of Crazy Us* is a dystopian film that mixes all of the above, as who you are today doesn't define who you will be tomorrow. Astute cinephiles would agree that this artistic project can't be explained with simple and reductive words – imagine a silent film. No one and nothing can be put in a box. It's a beautiful chaos that only a few can understand. Meet the hypersensitive, the genius in a bottle, the misunderstood.

But sorry, I digress; count me among those self-diagnosed ADHders, please.

We wondered how we got there, so let's get to the point.

Welcome to Planet X, the not-so-hypothetical hidden ninth planet (Planet 9) of the outer Solar system.

Astronomers based on Planet Earth are yet to prove the existence of this distant planet circling the Sun on a highly elongated path. Their assumption is that a theoretical Planet X explains unique gravitational patterns of stellar objects in the far-off region of icy debris, named the Kuiper Belt.

Planet 9 used to be Pluto for Earthlings until it was reclassified as a dwarf planet and then degraded as a non-planet by some. Poor Pluto *sob sob*.

My beautiful Planet X is indeed not a dwarf; it's a giant. Until further notice, it's a solid planet endowed with an atmosphere and composed of rock, silicate, water, and carbon. I'll let know-it-all Earthlings tell *me* it can only be a Jovian-like planet just 1.5 times the size of Earth.

Earth-based scientists conducting thorough research think they know better but have yet to find me and Planet X. Honestly, I'm not sure anyone on my planet wants to be discovered by Earthlings or vice versa. Adding Earthlings to an already crazy planet might lead to its downfall, especially after the past year. That said, Earthlings would be surprised by how similar both worlds are. We share kindred values, beliefs, stellar deities, and culture.

The inhabitants of Planet X belong to one race and are called Xians. Most are what Earthlings call humanoids; some have used medical progress to add extraordinary features to their bodies.

It's funny how science geniuses made mutations possible while the most basic diseases are still burgeoning. Conspiracy theorists would tell you their hiding of cures is a way to better control minions and the underprivileged.

I heard dragons and dinosaurs are extinct on Planet Earth, but that is not the case here, for better or worse.

Innumerable, marvellous animals populate seas and lands, clothed with heterogeneous coats like those on Earth.

Similarly, Xians' skin color palette is as diverse as a rainbow and depends on the exposition to the remote Sun, other stars and purple rains. These inconsequential differences among Xians have regrettably caused persecutions and genocides. We are not perfect, and our history is a testament to our imperfect actions.

I've been told that Xian means spiritually immortal celestial beings on Earth. It couldn't be more accurate and representative of who we are on Planet X – to an extent.

Planet X's Sphere is divided into four regions, reminiscent of Earth's Cartesian quadrant system, where each quarter Sphere's co-ordinates are Region I (+; +), Region II (–; +), Region III (–; –), and Region IV (+; –).

These Regions are subdivided into Lands similar to ancient realms on Planet Earth, where there are major cities and smaller ones. Each Land, led by a representative or a leader, has its own ruling system. Some Lands have additional titles and ruling particularities, like Great Banter Land. However, Xians couldn't care less about these ruling differences. What matters and what they keep arguing about is which Land is the most powerful. It doesn't serve the plot, but let's present the Top 3 and list the prime contenders.

Last time I checked, Invictus Land (–; +) – the cradle of Invictans led by The Turtle – was the most powerful. To be more accurate, it's a Federation – an aggregation of formerly separate Lands. Some 150 years ago, the 13 independent Lands signed *The Constitution Treaty*, gathered into a "Union," and became the United Lands of Invictus (in short, ULI). Another shorter form commonly used is Invictus Land or just Invictus. Its etymology means undefeated, unconquerable. The history of the powerful and massive Invictus Land confirms its repu-tation as a ruthless Empire and a Promised Land for all dreamers.

Next on the list is Red Dragon Land, the cradle of Dragonese led by the Red Dragon Party's representative – The Giant Red Panda. If you love an underdog story, you will adore this one from Region I (+; +). Despite significant obstacles, this Land reformed and renewed itself some 50 years ago to become a staple of Planet X's power game. Driven by industrial production and export-oriented manufacturing, it increased its investments and underwent market-oriented economic reforms, increasing its productivity significantly. It has one of the largest populations, making its workforce an extraordinary advantage. Powerful but discrete, Red Dragon Land operates judiciously and cautiously, hence its nickname – the Dormant Giant.

In third position, we have the most feared, Triple-Headed Golden Eagle Land (in short, Golden Eagle Land or Eagle Land), the cradle of Goldians led by The Libra. The vast Eagle Land (+; +) is one of its kind. Some might call it famous; some might call it infamous, but everybody whispers its name. Eagle Land has a rich culture and a resilient population. They look up to The Libra, who fears no one and nothing, who's ready to expand when necessary, and who is immune to threats – respect.

Let's not forget Hope Union (+; +), close to where I live, a coalition of Lands similar to Invictus Land, but where each Land remains sovereign as it's not a Federation. Among the most important players within Hope Union are Geranium Land, Frawn Land, Italic Land, and Bull Land.

For a long time, Hope Union (or HU) was Invictus' leading trading partner and its defense ally. Their alliance became official when both joined the North Xhui Treaty Organisation. Currently, both parties hesitate to remain in the coalition.

Among other power players is Cherry Land (+; −), the cradle of Cherrynese led by The Fox.

I would need a week to name all remaining Lands. Unfortunately, this is not Planet X's geography book. We will discover relevant Lands incrementally.

My planet is mostly at peace, but ancient rivalries and the current battle for supremacy weaken tranquility. Like on Earth, in every aspect, some are pleased with what they have, and some want... MORE! A good example would be the money chase in which everyone willingly participates.

At least all Planet X leaders agreed to shut down the Forex market to create a single monetary system with one cryptocurrency for the whole world – the Xi (ξ). Skeptic economists convinced them to keep precious metal coins as an alternative to distribute the Xi, fearing an unsolvable situation in case of a financial crash. Never mind, the Xi helped little, as economic inequalities between Lands and wealth disparities among Xians still thrive. Indeed, it helped preserve Planet X's stability from a macroeconomic point of view, but on the microeconomic level, nothing changed. While some people struggle to eat, xillionaires (equivalent to Earth's millionaires) and zillionaires (equivalent to Earth's billionaires) participate in witch hunts, power games, and sausage-eating competitions. Of course, there are some charitable acts, and I'm being reductive about their endeavors; I always tend to embellish stories.

Technologically, we are slightly more advanced than Earth is, but I won't disclose our engineering prowess. Earth is still at the beginning of the deep learning revolution, but let's just pretend we are at the same technological stage, tied up through quantum entanglement. Why? We are more spiritually developed, and we know what Earthlings will do with a more advanced technology: weaponize it and ultimately destroy their planet.

Earthlings who believe that a new industrial revolution would free them from their jobs would be disappointed to know that the majority still work on Planet X.

Consensus had been reached among all Planet X leaders to find a way to release all Xians from the workforce, replacing them with machines. Left to their fates and blinded by nostalgia, Xians failed to meet their needs and rose to get back to the ancient system. Xians succeeded, meaning we are back to Lands' leaders and big corporations dictating our future. We have what we asked for: jobs that are more or less meaningful, valuable, and debilitating. Upon our request, the three-sector model in economics is back on track and here to stay. Therefore, the long-forgotten 9 to 5 made its generalized comeback in our technologically advanced civilization. No, it's not exploitation this time; it's a choice made by most Xians who may now regret it.

To escape our monotonous lives and setbacks, we apply the same ancient methods: entertainment – sport, music, cinema, and other forms of art.

Centuries of research revealed that strong and secure social connections foster happiness, health, and longevity. That's why social media still exists despite us being ahead of time.

I only plug in for positive and informative connections.

The most famous one is the Xieta Verse. Created a few years ago by former tech competitors, it's a groundbreaking Invictan conglomerate, made available worldwide.

For nonconformists, there's an alternative to the Xieta Verse under construction: TacTic. It's a merger between the top Dragonese social media platforms.

Regarding video content, we have MeTube, a participative platform owned by the people. Diverse content creators who foster MeTube's eminence are called MeTubers.

There's also Chillflix, which dominates the online streaming-and-chat industry, whether it's serious projects like momentous films or frivolous reality TV shows.

I mostly use the Xieta Verse, which has pros and cons. When you feel alone or down, chances are you can find support from someone who experiences similar hardships, and you can find a silly thing that will make you feel better.

Of course, it is always better to use with caution. Some people are born malicious, and the nicest are the easiest targets. Not everyone will like you on the Xieta Verse, so people should favor real-life interactions instead of virtual ones and try not to seek strangers' approval. I might be doomed.

Anyway, what a pity Xieta Verse's founders haven't yet discovered a way for consumers to command their feed. At least they made up for it with the *Stuff Your Planet Months* program that allows us to connect to otherworldly social media platforms for a limited time when our planet's alignment allows it. That's how I learned everything I know about Earth. My only issue is that prograde motion always tends to shift my mood and colors.

For you to better understand my story, I translated my dialect (Xianese) into the most spoken language on Earth, English. I transcribed foreign idioms using the closest tellurian one.

In this opus, X-world will be the world, Planet X's X-men will be men, X-women will be women, and X will be... X. Sometimes, you can't work around untranslatability. For instance, some names could only find their translation using animals or myth references.

Beings from other planets will also be referenced as Aliens. On planet X, we are not at our first Alien encounter, and likely not at our last. These not-so-mysterious creatures easy come and easy leave back to their world, always.

Beware, Planet X has four Moons, and each might just be referenced as "the Moon" for easier understanding.

Xian calendar is based on our Moons' cycles, with 13 months in XX24. I translated the first 12 using the Earth system as it's incredibly similar. The most accurate translation for the last month of XX23 is Remember, and this year's 13th month is Dreizember.

Time dilatation theory might help you understand these relative differences – or not. I can only say that our hours, days, months, and years have different lengths than Earth's, and they change yearly.

Time is running out.

We've reached the end of year XX24 on Planet X, and it seems like nothing has changed for me. Big hug to those who can relate!

Even worse, while reading my Notes-to-self Journal, I realized that I always paired every step forward I made with two steps back.

For those who managed to do more than a 360°, congratulations. We'll buy your advice books and listen to your podcasts: "Doers vs. Thinkers, Active vs. Passive, Accountability vs. Victimhood, etc."

Yeah, I'm not *gonna* lie; I feel nauseous, too.

But how did we all get here?

If my quantum data is correct for those living on Earth, you just wrapped the year 2024.

What did it look like for you? Did you have time to process your feelings? Did you jump into the New Year with your emotional baggage despite knowing fully well you may never have the time to open it as you have already started to fill a new one?

What retrospective movie are you watching now? Are you the main character, a supporting role, an extra, the viewer, or just little old you?

What retrospective playlist are you listening to? Are you the producer, the songwriter, the singer, someone who works in the shadow, or just little old you?

Let's return to this companion, *Wrapping XX24*, where we will navigate my XX24 recap.

Welcome to my messed-up head, full of memories, thoughts, and fantasy news that neither you nor I have control of.

This is my life, yours, ours – a reflection on the past year, movie-making style shouting: "XX24, it's a wrap!"

When all our stories intertwine, we realize we are just one.

Let's all try to tell our delusional anecdotes.

I'll start.

Remember

H ERE WE ARE... WATCHING.

Like the importance of finding patient zero in an epidemic, remembrance allows us to glimpse what was on Xians' minds while at the intersection between a year and a change.

There were signs, but no one wanted to see what was before us. Due to normalcy bias, precursors noticing the patterns of a catastrophe in the making are called alarmists and overreactors, and the first whistleblowers are usually called crazy. Thus, everybody was watching – hoping for the best.

What are we even talking about? I wish I knew. Maybe we are trying to understand the year XX24 by looking at how XX23 ended.

***

Interesting news from Invictus Land: *New Dork Tales Magazine*'s Person of the Year XX23 is Mrs. Invictana Smart.

The title of the annual article is clear: "It's her world, and we're living in it." Who is she, anyway? Ugh.

She reminds me of someone with her short lavender hair and brown eyes... Wait!

Is that my middle school classmate who was serenading her made-up boyfriend from her bedroom window? Having her glasses on but still unable to see, he didn't belong to her? YOU, Stalker... or Lover might be more appropriate for youngsters? In any case, good memories.

I remember reenacting her first play in drama class. She started to chase her dreams so young!

Time flies; wow, she made it bigger than my hometown. She's now one of the world's most renowned playwrights, composer, and stage theatre actress. Some would say, "She's the theatre industry" because she's breaking records even faster than she was driving her first car – the infamous white *Growler* SUV.

She's currently on an immersive theatre world tour named *The Auras*. *The Auras* is a second-hand mastermind idea, a patchwork of all her plays, combining her Arena Theatre plays with her Dance and Musical Theatre acts. Incredibly diverse, considering that she has composed and produced countless plays covering genres like chamber theatre, tragedy, comedy, drama, puppetry, and ballet. I guess she was inspired by the latter for her *Tales Magazine* cover, from which I infer she's a black cat mother now.

Fun fact: since I read that special edition about Mrs. Invictana, I have unwanted information about her flooding my Xieta Verse feed, and everything I know now is against my will.

Where was I? Out of this bubble, that's for sure because there's a lot more happening at the moment. Let's pop it and see where it goes, hoping it won't break my heart like Huge Grit did.

The most talked-about news is that she got herself a Wild Valentine, a loving, happy, loud, and proud Valentine. It almost feels like she manifested him as he comes right after her last play titled *Stalker*. The good-looking man has been a theater fan and has praised her drama plays his whole life. Weird? No... Cute!

The chemistry is obvious, and the alchemy is glaring, but some people are clutching their pearls, even if it's not their business. Who are they? Well, her theatre fans – xillions of them. They consider Mrs. Smart their creative mother and go by the name Smarties. They also named each theatrical performance of *The Auras* – Smarties parties. But before they cover me with sparkling attacks for not knowing everything about their adored Mrs. Smart – little confession: I have been living as a recluse lately.

Another hurtful confession: I sometimes separate art from the artist. For example, I love a good signature cocktail: put ingredients in, mix it, shake it off, and drink it – no questions asked to the bartender. Just pour it and fill my glass; I'll do the rest without knowing the drink's name or the mixologist who just made it. If asked what I'm drinking, I'll make up something, which is easy.

Please put your mind at rest. I'm trying to change that, as I know I'm risking getting myself in dire straits while unintentionally supporting the worst. When it matters, I willingly remove the spice and edge to my life that's becoming more bland. My mom would say mocktails are better for health, anyway.

What follows is the last disclaimer: if you have addictions, please stop reading this as it's highly addictive. I put sugar into all my words. Thus, if you can't afford the magic potion of Oze, please get in touch with health magicians or the real-life dedicated hotline.

***

Speaking of hot sugar, straight from Frawn Land, Frawnch actor Thym Chalumeau is in theaters again, starring in *Willi Winkatt*.

It's the story of a candy shop owner who got shot because he was letting customers lick lollipops for an appreciated ξ60 Cents – no fruity or zesty flavors, unfortunately. He miraculously survived, and he's still a hustler whose only ambition is to get rich or to die hoping. In the meantime, he enjoys life and pops his *King Path* sparkling wine or a whisky bottle every night in the club. So Frawnch, I won't lie; this is my style. Too bad I don't have enough money for one-on-one fun with him; I would have taken him shopping and asked him to party with me.

Other news mash-up: Deluwood is nominating the best movies (*Open-Namer*, *Dollbie*, and *Rich Things*, among others) for the next O'Stars (Academy rewarding the best in the industry, mostly known for its lavish award ceremony). Congratulations to all nominees!

***

On the opposite side of the planet, we hear about a conflict escalating in Holy Land. Holy Land is a sacred Land led by two rivals where blurred border lines, beliefs, and valuable assets continuously spark wars and conflicts.

Who started? I don't know, and I'm already trying to remember the names of the two rivals. I recall hearing about a cultural festival ending in a massacre earlier this year. As a highly empathetic Xian, I find this calamity heart-wrenching and beyond understanding.

Then retaliations happened, and by the end of XX23, thousands of people were sadly caught in the crossfire.

Some say that conflict started way before, at the origin of Xian life, but I lack knowledge in the matter, and it's not the subject of this simple, silly manuscript anyway.

***

Speaking of debates, Invictus Land's former leader, known as The Phoenix (or The Orangutan, per his critics), is losing his wings. The Invictan Big Three Court just announced that he might never be able to run or fly. People thought he had moved on from his ambition to rule Invictus Land and the world.

Try again; he fires people, not the other way around. He's ready to fight them all; we can expect endless back and forth until he gets a resolution. He's one in 13 zillion, yet convinced he's more than just *A Man*.

I'm pretty sure he peacefully watches *The CEOs* every year as a retrospective movie. What follows might help us understand why... or not.

***

It's my favorite time of the year, and we haven't had a lot of joy lately. There is nothing better than a chucklesome *Led Talk* podcast to lift my spirit before the New Year, with my favorite – the one and only, Gabe Churchelle. I like to call him Gabe as if we were real-life friends. I can be delusional, too, sometimes.

He's the only man on Planet X who can walk away from ξ50 xillion and live to tell the tale at a Dame O'Purple opera. On his last podcast episode of the year, Gabe discusses the power of dreams and hopes that put boundaries to the test. It takes one wishful thinker to recognize one, and I always tend to be aligned with the green-eyed man.

I didn't need to be called out and put on blast like that. Luckily, he doesn't know me and does not talk about me, but I feel attacked when he keeps repeating that line: "The weakest dream loses."

He then recounts the story of Bunny, his childhood classmate. Bunny was the archetypal perfect child who dreamed of becoming a Land leader, and everybody could picture him making that dream come true.

By an unanticipated turn of events, Bunny ended up with a humbling and essential job at a retail store.

Here's an extract from the podcast transcript:

"At sixteen years old, Bunny and his first love discovered they had a bun in the oven. We don't have time to get into the recipe – but when two became three, the distressed man bet on himself and started a board game company. Surprisingly, it became a flourishing company that changed his destiny. Enamored, his wife turned the company's flagship game – the hangman, into a jewelry line. It got even more successful when Beanie Haylish – the famous Invictan fortune teller known for eating spiders – rocked the "H" necklace for her live psychic reading sessions, making it a number-one seller. They started from the bottom, but thanks to their dreams, they'll live happily ever after, just like Big Gas X, my other childhood classmate who fulfilled his dream of becoming a wildland firefighter."

Gabe is letting his guard down as usual and the jokester's podcast session made me smile. Ok, I'm weak, I laughed.

Perhaps end-of-year magic, when closing the show, Gabe exhibits an extreme seriousness – a first, since he started his podcast venture 37 years ago when he was only 22.

Like Gabe, many people seem to remember something important happening to them when they were 22. I've tried to walk down memory lane, *and surprise* I felt like a total failure at 22!

What's soothing is that I remember I still had dreams and hopes. If I had the burning fire in me right now, I would have fought more for them back then – the same way Gabe fought his podcast co-host, who jumped him after losing his mind earlier this month.

Luckily, in attendance, his cowboy friend James Djanger came to his defense while Gabe's security was struggling not to slip on the oily floor with their fancy shoes. James Djanger got confused by his clone, so someone else had to step in and save the day: The Dandy.

The Dandy is a famous Invictan puppeteer attending the podcast as a guest before all this mess. Used to the oily scene, he had the appropriate combat shoes to de-escalate the situation and even celebrate the win with his signature dance. The Dandy helped neutralize the assailant and saved Gabe from great danger. Not all heroes wear capes.

Gabe was furious and now remembers wondering why the floors were oily. A private investigation graciously offered by The Dandy revealed that the wooden floor had been covered with linseed oil to "enhance its color and protect it from wear." They are yet to find the floor treatment company to understand why they didn't put any warning cones. You know, the usual ones with signs indicating 'Caution Wet Floor' or 'Warning, possible risk of slip conditions.'

But Gabe wants to move on. He doesn't want to make himself into a victim, and he shows empathy for his co-host, who allegedly snapped because of money issues that made him homeless.

We live, and we learn. No one knew what the man was going through, just like no one knows what's going into people's minds, and no one knows what's in the Treasured Safe.

At least we know what's in Gabe's vault. Before the final punchline, we learn that Gabe gave his vault's key to his wife, and she was disappointed to find out what was inside: a Video Home System. That VHS is the recording of unreleased sessions of the *Led Talk* podcast. Considering Gabe's craftsmanship, this is a golden goose that will help bring fortune to his family in case of need. No cash, having to understand the hidden message and work on the perfect delivery; that's the beauty and the irony of it. At least *they* have a backup plan!

I don't have one, but I can't complain; I had a fantastic XX23!

I may have brushed some feelings, but broadly, I had a blast!

Happy, healthy, living, traveling, in a relationship with Bae * #couplegoal *, not so many family disagreements, and a mid-paying partially-remote corporate job as a Chief Happiness Officer at The Xherkin. What else can I ask for?

Bae doesn't want me to be overly public about our relationship, but it's perfect; I'm not one to post on the Xieta Verse anyway. I'm a self-diagnosed neurodivergent introvert, and we only see each other at my place, just perfection!

However, because of Gabe, I wonder if I'm living *the* dream.

Do I want Bae to propose to me? Should I get married and have kids asap? Maybe it wasn't a good idea to listen to that podcast.

I felt exceptionally well, and now it keeps ringing:

"The weakest dream loses."

What's *my* dream? Did I ever have a dream? Am I winning?

Do I even want to win?

If not, am I okay with being considered a loser?

My dilemma reminds me of something my late friend Matt Chan used to say: "People need to fulfill all their dreams for them to know if there were the right dreams to have."

Matt departed Planet X to explore faraway stars and share his poetry eternally. Before leaving, Matt made me promise never to give up, always fight back, and most importantly, enjoy life.

I'm left to question why the wisest poets always leave us when we least expect it and we most need them.

I would hate to break my promises to Matt, so let's find ourselves a good scenery to start the New Year. No one needs to ask me twice to hop on a supersonic plane.

***

Here I come, Invictus Land's Tales City, the cradle of Talers.

My friends and I call it Rumor City.

Like a skin-walker merging into local culture, I get used to the fast-paced grind, whispering "he said, she said," shouting "I'm in a hurry!" and adding "dead-ass serious" randomly in sentences.

I heard it looks like Earth's Big Apple, a city that never sleeps with skyscrapers, lemon taxis, busy streets, creativity, and a nice beat in the back of my mind. Welcome to the state where Empires run the show. My bank account has a negative balance, but I agree with Talers that "money *ain't* a thing."

I already feel at home, walking next to people who are so ambitious that I think I can be the next financial market wolf, too. Looking at the moving Invictan flag in front of the Money Building, I'm becoming a fearless girl, too. Whether or not I stay here, from now on, I'll take the bull by the horns and grab the bear by the tail.

It feels like a dream. Everything is vibrant, and my introverted self is even enjoying party life. You don't know me, even so, you would not recognize tipsy me when I mingle with random troublemakers, looking for the next best speakeasy and spending my rent money on rooftops' delicacies.

I'm having a blast, even if traffic jams are terrible, as ever. While my ride is at a standstill, I observe Talers. Everyone is busy minding their business in humble neighborhoods in Tales City, and I like it. Talers' chutzpah is so charming and conversations in the streets go like this:

"That's real estate mogul Jane Loe's residence to the left. Lovely penthouse, fun times – no cap!"

"Yeet! That's tabloid mogul Rumor Girl's hotel to the right, the place to be for the A-list girl squad, pick-me Mollys, and star-struck wannabees."

"You said what you said! That's on the same block as the Mean Girls' recording studio. Let's walk away and stay away from music."

I always listen to Talers' advice.

Frolicking in Neutral Park and playing with squirrels is way more interesting; the greenery is just unworldly. Sitting on a stranger's dedicated bench, eating strawberries and pickles, drinking wine, following my guts, and drunk-dialing my ex to empty my iron heart.

The coward didn't pick up, so I left a voicemail:

"All the love I gave you will never equal to the love you'll have. Distance and time are not why we broke up; your non-stop gaslighting is. Idiot!"

Good idea. And before you go there, no, I'm not jealous of my ex's newfound love. I don't want him back; I'm logically funnier and happier without him. I moved on.

Pickles left a sour taste in my mouth, but let's get back to Remember's beauty and smile.

On the last day of XX23 – New Year's Eve, I'm wishful drinking before I carry through my promise to make January a dry month.

Even if I don't get the rom-com movie kiss at midnight, I'm ready to cross the yearly bridge.

I don't consider myself a romantic, but Bae disappearing at the only moment that matters ruined it. Without the fireworks, it would have been sweet nothing! Where was he? It's still a mystery that he and his opened zipper haven't managed to clarify to this day. He's losing me.

At least I could count on the single ladies to dance with me during his absence. I don't recall the name of the free-spirited one with the pink dress who was shouting while slurring her words a bit: "Sparkly dress on, sparkling wine, sparkling eyes, and sparkling skies, but not lucky with the hot guys!"

Let's enjoy the dance and the folklore. May we all go with the flow in the coming year.

The future can only be bright. I'm a good, good girl; good karma can only follow.

Many blessings!
See you next year!

In the meantime, here I am... still watching.

1

January

H ERE WE ARE... HOPING.

New Year's Resolutions Month!

XX24.

Let's go, or like Wild Valentine would say, "Let's *Fluffing* Go!"

This year is going to be MY year! I can feel it. I don't want to lose; only big dreams and high hopes are allowed. I am ready to reclaim my life and make it the best year I have ever had.

I'm tired of being the underdog; I want to be a hero, not the anti.

Time to set goals, make wishes, promises, and resolutions: dry January, hit the gym, better manage finances (whatever 50/30/20 and 30/30/40 mean), be more vocal, adjust my kind/clever balance, fall in love, feel free, write a song and 99 more delusional plans.

***

While cruising in the Sulley River, let's wave to a fellow green lady, the Statue of Freedom. Here she is in Upper Taler Bay, magnificent under the sunset. Just like me, avoiding dangerous dark days and hoping that one day we'll achieve our craziest dreams. It might not be too little too late, and we should never say never. Maybe this year, I'll feel like her: a mix between a divinity, a peasant, and my unlimited imagination.

Without speaking, the fiery lady is inspiring and reminding me of my favorite pose when I was younger; when I still had a voice.

When I return home, maybe I should find my old fighting spirit and ask for a salary raise and a promotion. Can I get it? Sure! You can take it all when your mindset shifts, and anything can happen. Goodbye, open space, and small talk. Hello, private office, leather swivels, and turning tables. In the meantime, let's have fun and cheer us up.

***

Tales City's Brothay Street: let's take pictures with Deluwood home-made wax figures like Tim Crazy, Bros Willing, Lady Mama, Lehoe Dicabravo, Timmy Fallen, Marilean, the Recollection Queen or Duane 'The Stone' Hotson.

I'm bored, let's try a musical. *Jasmin Tea* is playing. It's splendid! So good! If Mr. Eagleheart were in my life, I would wake up smiling like in the commercials. I would never complain, not a single day.

Ok, let's not exaggerate.

A little confession: while watching the show, I can't help but make my wish to the genie in the jar; "Healthy year for all and peace in the world." Look at me, feeling myself. I don't have the looks of a pageant, but the speech is ready. In my mom's womb, I heard that fire burns and pretty hurts, so I chose the brain. That was the first wrong decision of a xillion that followed. Anyway, it was a great night!

***

When I return to my Upper Feast Side hotel, I scroll on the Xieta Verse and learn that an earthquake struck Cherry Land. Here I am, sorry for their losses, wondering why this world is so cruel. I wanted less empathy for things I can't control, but I can't help it; I still care too much.

My sickening gentleness keeps me from enjoying anything for the rest of the night. I go to the bar and ask for a cocktail, then two, and after that, I stop counting. Should the first day count for the dry month?

You might call me self-centered, but I think that maybe those two wishes ruined everything for everyone in January, and I'm now hoping it won't mess up the whole year XX24.

For those wondering, I checked; the Cherry Land's earthquake happened before I made those wishes. I promise it wasn't me; I'm not the problem, and the plane incident that occurred in the same place the next day is not my fault either.

***

Thinking about planes, a few days later, the world is booing Blooming – a supersonic jetliner manufacturer, as part of an Invictan Airline's plane fuselage just blew out midair. I read about all that while sitting in the boarding lounge at the airport before my return flight, which used the same supersonic plane model. Isn't that ironic? You ought to know.

More seriously, remember what I said about first whistleblowers? Now, our dear Sir Garnet, who started pointing out safety issues years ago, is heard and believed. Other informants raising concerns about the newly developed Supersonic Butterflies and the increasing airspace traffic are yet to be considered truthful. Supersonic Butterflies with their flapping wings are the future of aviation, an innovative form of flying that is even more advanced than the more common supersonic planes. What could go wrong?

***

As for me, it's time to say: "Bye, Bye, Bye Tales City!"

I'm not good, but I'm going home, back to black, back to my workaholic life, and rehab is not even an option; I have bills to pay. The best is coming.

Let's be a fighter like Golden Sparrow Land's flying soldiers. I might be Miny this year, surrounded by my besties, Taz and Baz. I'll finally free Patzy from the boyfriend zone and officially become his Lady. Let's hope it's not just utopia and precious illusions sold by Wow-lywood, Golden Sparrow's movie industry. With their 6-hour-long romantic movies with the wind as a paid actor, if anyone can pretend to have taken part in love invention, it's them!

I've never visited Golden Sparrow Land, located in Region IV (+; −), the cradle of Spandians led by The Mammoth and The Moose. I would love to visit this colorful and culturally rich Land as soon as it becomes safer for *Strī, Aurat* and *Mahilā*.

Without counting my culinary experiences, the closest I've been to Spandians is through the phone, thanks to companies' call center relocations. I remember receiving a call from an after-sales officer from *The Jungle* (an online market store founded by one of the Xieta Verse's fathers − El Jefe) after declaring an incident.

The phone number was seemingly from Viking Land (+; +) and the conversation was fantastic:

"Good morning. My name is Giovanni, and I'm calling to inform you that I can't do anything to solve your issue, Madam," he said with the strongest Spandian accent.

"Are you sure you're calling from Viking Land, Giovanni?

Because... I don't want to sound cliché, but Giovanni? Like an Italic Land Giovanni?" I replied.

"If you don't have any questions, I will close your request. Please stay online for the satisfaction survey," Giovanni added.

"What The *Fluff*! No, I'm not *fluffing* satisfied! I need you to solve my *fluffing* issue!" I screamed.

"Please don't use profanity just because you're unsatisfied, Madam. What's the difference between an unhappy customer and a dog?" He asked.

"Are you asking ME the *fluffing* question? I'm going to have a heart attack, I swear, my *fluffing*..."

"The answer is: eventually, the dog will stop barking. If you're not peeling well like the banana, you should go to the doctor." He interjected, before hanging up.

I was left speechless. I was so mad, but ended up chuckling despite the stupidity of Giovanni's joke, that perfectly matched the stupidity of my first question.

I love Spandians; they're one of the funniest people. I told you, I'm easily amused, and I will always fall into the daddy's joke trap. My Xieta Verse friend's husband would ask me to shut the trapdoor on that nonsense. Wrong year, I'm not ready to close any door; let's open them all!

The only thing I should try to close is my mouth, though. I keep forgetting I'm supposed to give abstinence a try.

Speaking of food, that's another praiseworthy quality of Golden Sparrow Land, its edibles. Put me in front of a Beamyani rice, a Tippi Messali, a cheese Paan, or a Malak Maneer, and I will forget the diet I never started. Delicious! Spicily delicious. Don't forget the Lassy on the side, or the pill will be hard to swallow.

***

I hope the good old poker patriot Ball Chicbelly had ordered a Lassy just before parting ways with his NSL (New Stud League) team.

NSL is a new stud poker tournament only held in Invictus Land's humongous poker stadiums, hence its famous slogan, "New Fairytale Life." The 13 Invictan Lands are split into regional divisions in which poker teams face each other throughout the year in rounds. NSL yearly finals are one of the most significant events in Invictus Land, reuniting the "who's who" of "pay what?" and celebrated with a Super Masked Ball (SMB).

I guess that Ball Chicbelly won't attend the SMB party anymore. Indeed, the veteran turned NSL coach might have other plans after spending over 20 years servicing Bean City's team (Northeastern Invictus). With Bean City's star player Tim Broady, he helped his team win countless trophies. But it's over.

As the saying goes: "Everything that has a beginning has an end."

Fun fact: Wild Valentine is an NSL poker player who is among the best. Brains and beauty, Mrs. Invictana knew what her criteria were, and the boy crossed them all. Yeah, she got what she wanted.

Just a trivial issue: NSL is a male-dominant world, and Dads, Vlads, and Conrads are not extremely happy to see her around cheering for her man on her days off from theatre. Some judgy Judys even join in criticizing her support for her boyfriend, calling it "a manufactured, attention-seeking PR (Public Relations) move." Mrs. Invictana is reportedly thinking "it's not very girl's girl of them" and writing her next play, *Revenge*.

***

Day 3, Invictus Land's Deluwood is shaking and trembling.

Originally, Deluwood was the name given to the entertainment industry in Angels City, but it has since been used to refer to the entire Invictan entertainment industry.

The measurement of P-waves and S-waves pinpoints the earthquake's epicenter at Angel City's studio zone. More precisely, the first foreshocks originate from Shayle's stage set, when the real-life Willi Winkatt sat on his leather couch to spit facts and dare anyone to pass their gnarled fingers in his luscious organic hair.

Shayle is hosting a TV game show called *The Truth or The Leash*. I've never understood the rules, but all I know is that Willi Winkatt wants to set the records straight, and it seems inevitable that – quoting Blessed Luke: "Nothing is covered up that will not be revealed or hidden that will not be known."

Shayle starts by saying, "Willi can't walk away from ⚡50 xillions a fifth time. To the people who stole his jokes, please give it back so that he can move on with his life – me too."

The rest of the game is all over the place, more disorganized than my hoarded house. It goes from name-calling and click-baiting to the Illuminance conspiracy theories linking alleged cross-dressers.

Good Lord, Willi Winkatt is telling us to protect our wormholes, too, and his predictions for year XX24 are going more viral than the Batvid-19 pandemic and its Lableak-20 variant.

Now, if we're messing with astronomy, I listen. But I can't unsee it, I can't unhear it – I feel like he just opened the wrong portal in the universe. Our closed portal protects us from unwanted Alien invasions, and we always want it that way.

Oh My, Shayle is shocked, drinking us all underneath the table over there, except for me. I made it through that crazy TV-game night without stumbling! Not proud, but honest. Be reassured, the savage years are long gone since I turned 21.

We must admit that we all remembered one lesson from this: "If The Dandy wants to party, you have to say no!" It's not as if I could bump into him on my way to work, but thanks for the tip!

I know that the funny bartender, Kenny Hard, mentioned in all this mess would have preferred to be lifted out of this and peacefully enjoy his breakfast at *Stiffannie's*. The upside is that we heard him talk to his buddy, M.D. Ludi, in the latter's medical podcast studio. M.D. Ludi for sure thinks Willi is acting like a fool and should check his temperature – doctor's orders!

***

I should also check my temperature right now. I am submerging into my chronicles instead of thinking about my next strategy to climb up the corporate ladder, especially since chances are that my story will only find its relevance 10,000 years after being buried in the wild jungle.

Why not choose the word "bear" as the passcode to open the strongbox explaining Xian life to people in the future? The first lines read: "If it's brown, lay down – if it's black, fight back – if it's white, say goodnight. Just choose one; it'll always be the best choice you made in your life."

I wonder if Her Empress Magnificent II gave similar wise advice to her son, His Emperor Ritzy X, before abdicating. Her Empress Magnificent II is the last sovereign of Cookie Land, part of Hope Union, and the cradle of Cookanes. I may never know private conversations between the matriarch and her son, but I'll take the cookies and the king cake recipes any day. Maybe the fusion food chef Jordy, known for his sharp stallion, will share them one day.

* I trust you, Jordy, come closer and let us all know! *

I keep forgetting I'm supposed to hit the gym and apply a calorie deficit.

As I warned, no one should expect any life coaching tips here. You're still on your own to fix your heartbreak and your weight-loss plateau; you'll always be.

"Is it that complicated?"

"Yes, it is."

Sometimes, I swear, it's just another nightmare after the other. But I have a whole year; I'm old enough to own my decisions. Like Sam – my Frawnch friend – would say, "I'm A Major and vaccinated."

***

Mid-January, it is time to start *SYTYCR* (So You Think You Can Rule), a TV game show created a few years back in partnership with the Xieta Verse, aimed at facilitating the vote for Invictus Land's leader. Indeed, after the debacle caused by the elections five years ago, Invictans voted for the *SYTYCR* system as the TV show allows them to have more decisive content about the leading contenders in the ruling race and is more entertaining.

The show starts with a Happy Families-style game to decide who is running for each party and then goes on with other games we will discover later.

The main contestants for the leader position are two Invictan parties (or families) who rebranded their names this year for an unknown reason: if I'm not mistaken, Los Rojos (formerly known as The Reds) and Los Blaus (formerly known as The Blues).

On Los Rojos' side, The Phoenix (ULI's former leader) is rising from his ashes and wins the first happy families' feud. He's back for good. His fans promise he's the Savior, while his haters fear he will antagonize them.

On Los Blaus' side, The Turtle, the current leader, slowly but surely shows that he is ready for a second term. His fans promise "better him than his opponent," while his haters fear he will continue to forget where he is in the middle of a speech instead of retiring.

In Between Both, you have those contemplating these strange and green days. Let's trust The Process; being criticized can't define one's winning power. Some people disagree and are considering moving to Coma City, a mythical place where Xians use cryogenics to hibernate.

***

While Invictus Land is debating who's the best violinist in *SYTYCR's* music playoff, we got some worrying news from home in Great Banter Land.

For context, Great Banter Land was part of Hope Union for as long as I can remember until Grits recently voted for a Grexit. We're "outer than out" now. The particularity of GB Land is that we kept our ancient Monarchy system alongside the more modern ruling system led by an Optimister (currently The Ram) and relevant institutions.

His Highness The Unicorn is at the head of GB Monarchy (also known as The Company); he oversees not only GB Land but also faraway Lands and Islands that share the same sense of "identity, unity and pride" as per the *Seldom Wealth Treaty* they all signed.

Out of the blue, The Company informs us Grits that the beloved Kountess has been hospitalized. Her Grace The Kountess is the discreet wife of His Grace The Kount, heir to the GB Land's throne.

We don't know more yet, and we don't need to. Remember Talers' way, "If it's not about you, don't meddle."

Sometimes, you need to give it time. People should show respect, especially when they realize that one's life is dedicated to helping others at the expense of one's dreams. Some might say that the lack of privacy is the price of fame and money, while others say it's a tradition.

By good fortune, none of these concern me.

***

We're still in January, and the news doesn't get better; Holy Land's conflict is causing much damage.

Maze Strip, a small island on international waters close to Holy Land, is at the center of this conflict. Maze Strip was originally part of Mother Land until Holy Land's Lone Bue Star legion invaded it a few decades ago. Their on-again, off-again toxic relationship laid the foundations of an unstable geopolitical environment from which several conflicts originated – the most recent one dated XX23.

Despite constant wars and destructions, the people of Maze Strip, known as Mazestrinians, show incredible resilience and strength. Everyone hopes the conflict won't get to a point of no return, even if deep down, we know it's already too late.

Just like when Gisella La Madrina became a *clandestina*, she sealed her fate to emerge as one of the most feared medicine dealers ever. It's not a flex, as we all know how that story ends.

New fear unlocked: being caught in a crossfire.

***

A glimpse of joy in Cherry Land: Cherrynese are burning precious liquid gas and catching up on space technology. They reached the Moon for the first time. Let's hope they won't find flower killers on the dark side there. Anyway, congratulations!

***

Thinking about technology, I received a pop-up asking me to drink to Exron's health (one of Xieta Verse's founders), who announced he implanted a mic on someone's brain. I'm not even surprised and don't want to know more.

Mic drop!

Everybody is so creative; it's going to be a tremendous year.

***

XX24 is the year of the Wool Dragon.

Xians' New-Year animal changes annually on a 13-year cycle. On top of that, each animal has ten variants to represent ten elementary natural fabrics, including bamboo, cashmere, cotton, hemp, jute, leather, linen, silk, sisal, and wool.

Ancient myths recount that our calendar comes from 13 mythical animals who descended from above in a precise order to help Xians learn about crops and celebrate life. We don't have enough time to list all animals and dig deep into those myths, but what I can say is that the animal of the year sets the tone.

XX24's Wool Dragon is predicted to be a year of substantial change, evolution, and action. Got to get it, let's unleash it!

* Snap! * Smarties were hoping for the year of the Snake. I don't want to start a circus with the cute clowns, but XX25 is the year they might not be ready for. The big revelation might come...

Will *A* mother of SnakeS be up for the challenge, or should Smarties calm down instead of asking for sundry other treats?

Time will tell... or not.

I said the Wool Dragon's unveiling sets the pace, but I think the Invictan Big Two Court took the myth too far.

They're investigating TacTic (Red Dragon Land's beta version of the Xieta Verse) and its influence on Invictan lives. Rumors were that TacTic used dance and funny content to influence young Invictans and spy on Invictus Land's Big Corporations.

During a court hearing of TacTic's CEO, the Invictan prosecutor is asking the non-Dragonese if he's sure he's not Dragonese:

"Oh, you took a plane to come to court. Flying leads to dragonflies and dragon fruits eating.

Are you Dragonese, Sir?" is questioning the prosecutor.

"No, I'm not. Just like Mr Zu Burger, who is Invictan, I'm tired of sushi. I only eat fettuccini and zucchini," replied TacTic's CEO, bringing Mr. Zu Burger (one of the Xieta Verse's founders) into the debate.

Prosecutors allegedly even suggested that using a lighter once in your life automatically makes you a Dragonese that breathes fire.

I'm not a Xieta Verse expert, but I failed to understand the link and the relevance of TacTic CEO being Dragonese. If I had been clever enough to understand this topic, I wouldn't have considered this whole hearing a joke. I know it's not, but I lack knowledge.

***

I take nothing seriously. But even if I laugh, I'm sad at this stage.

History repeats itself. When I'm not laser-focused on my goals in the first month, they remain unachieved for the rest of the year.

It shouldn't be the case, but nothing hurts like the end of January when you haven't made one of your promised changes.

We never know what the future holds. While I feel stuck, the world keeps spinning madly on with those Smarties parties I don't quite understand. I may be missing another love that could heal me.

In the meantime, here I am... still hoping.

2

February

H ERE WE ARE... LOVING.

L.O.V.E all day, L.O.V.E all month!

I still want to escape my fate. The goal is to fall deep. One love, one life. Maybe I'll end up with my All-Time Crush.

Get used to it; this is me now.

If you want me to play that silly game, I would Kiss Bad Man, Marry Superb Man, Kill Madam WWW, and Tell Wonder Girl. Because, if I locate her, I swear I'll tell her I fell in love with the LinkOld Lawyer, too.

If he gives me a chance, *cruzemos los dedos*, we'll be one of those couples who wear matching hoodies.

No, I'm kidding. I'm not young enough for him, but I'm old enough to hire him! He's a good guy and taken; leave him alone, Judys!

O Valentine, Valentine, why are you, Valentine? *Why*, not *where* – the debate is closed.

Since one or a few crazy lunatics made it the month of love pollution a few centuries ago, let's love.

If I don't seem to grasp Xians' fascination about love, which is as overrated as the 300% markup on red roses and lingerie, I still can tolerate lovers who switch off their X Must lights in February. Those I can deal with.

This is my game; I set the rules. I can trade a maroon scarf for a tie-dye crewel, and the happy peasants would shout, "All hail the delicate Queen!" Maybe that's what all the tartan is about.

Oh no, *spoiler alert*, we're still stuck in February. What should we talk about instead?

All these perfumes, romantic movies, heart-shaped everything, and chocolate commercials make me want to find the man who will love every shade of me and make me realize what I'm missing. I know what I want, and I'll get it: *See* by Seely, the new scent that will make us "see each other."

You might wonder why I'm talking about finding genuine love when I already have Bae. Didn't I tell you it's over?

We are just one couple in zillions, and there are more breakups in January than in the rest of the year. They say personal growth has its roses and thorns. That said, the love cartel won. Now, I also want love to always win and my future soulmate's face to go from potato to tomato when he looks at me.

It's nothing I ever had or wanted, but I am ready for *us* and prepared for *him*.

***

While daydreaming about that hypothetical love, I learn from the Xieta Verse that Gan Peter – the bougie cheese grater's seller – is hissing at her archnemesis Pink Doll, the mukbang influencer. I forgot who won at the end; I guess neither did.

The only winning I remember from February is in sport, with Invictus' women binballers, who are getting more recognition. Among the greats, Kate-Lynn, the northern belle, is breaking records. Watch out; she might become *Tales Magazine*'s athlete of the year if she keeps up the majestic work.

***

Speaking of records, Smarties' mother hopped on her private supersonic plane like a kangaroo from Sunburnt Land. She made a grand entrance at the Granites – the ceremony rewarding any art form. I am such a fan of her look; it reminds me of my wild and prosperous days. She got herself some awards and made an announcement: "there won't be any *fluffing* snakes on the *fluffing* tiled plane for the next theatre plays." It seems Smarties have a better chance to witness an Alien abduction than a snake invasion.

Mrs. Invictana's next play is *PTSD: Tales of the Alive Poet Society*. It's always nice to meet a fellow self-proclaimed poet. No, that's just me. She's a recognized and chartered poet, right? If not yet, at least she didn't wait to vanish like the greats to have her title.

As usual, she's outsmarting everybody; I now understand why she's known to be the chess master or the rainmaker.

And we don't even know the magnitude of the *PTSD* play yet, as she exits the podium before revealing more.

***

At least this time, she's not interrupted by The Vulture, the problematic abstract artist whose evil regimen seems worse than a vampire's.

I am neutral here; I always try to find the good in everyone. They say "hurt people hurt people;" he might be scarred or crying for help.

The Vulture may not be as heartless as people think. Look at how lovey-dovey he is with his naked muse.

Also, remember, a "genius" is usually misunderstood. It doesn't excuse everything; I know. But we all know "legends" rarely beg for forgiveness, even if they should.

Anyway, I bet Mrs. Invictana is stronger and numb to it now; let's try to move on from the big elephant that just jumped on my mind.

***

Don't be surprised by my extreme sympathy; they say I was born wise, an old soul – always trying to learn and fixing on words like a magnet.

That's why The Jeydi's speech at the Granites moved me. Some say the movie director embarrassed his young lady, the famous actress Queen V – also known as Virgo Queen.

I beg to differ. Reflecting on it, he inspired me in a way, considering I am writing these words after an exhausting day at work. I've decided to keep showing up until I get the recognition I deserve.

Their love is also inspiring. It allegedly started when the pair met on the *Bony & Clide* movie set. The genius couple invented love and has been going strong for two decades after ups and downs, whether or not people like it.

***

Maybe one day I'll be called a genius too, the greatest of all. If I cut the comedy, being qualified as generous would be enough. Let's manifest *that*, at least! Until then, I have nothing to give, and nothing is enough.

I will not lie; I wasn't at peace with the little I had until recently. Experiencing loss, facing difficulties, and witnessing others' agony help mitigate what we go through.

Seeing the Grit gossip pioneer Windy Pettiams fight for her well-being, sanity, and life affects me. The only solace in her sad story is the support she's receiving from her friend White Shyna, her fans, and her family. It's another reminder that anything can happen – the good, the bad, a beginning or an end.

Note to self: *Carpe Diem* and stop to smell the roses, even if you have a pollen allergy.

***

What about little crazy us? Still on our own?

All my single birds, meet someone like you. "Hello from the same side!" I saved you a seat on the unfortunate bench. "Enchanted" (*curtsy*).

We can't stop dancing in the rain even if it's not raining men. Should we practice self-love and buy ourselves flowers like Smiley Girl told us? Let's put our hands in our pockets and throw our wild card, too! At least, that's one of the seven things I am made for.

I might be a lost cause; getting older but still too shy to say goodbye when the party's over, I doubt I'll ever have the courage to seize the love of my life. Let's pin a quote on our conspiracy board and reflect on it. It's the same result, and it's all about love.

***

You might start to know me more than myself.

What's the next step?

Find ourselves a magnificent scenery.

So, here I come, Frawn Land, the cradle of Frawnch (or more affectionately Frawnchies), led by The Bulldog. The Bulldog's romantasy story sparks heated debates in low tea rooms and sets the tone for anyone looking for passion. If the timeline of his love at first sight with his now-wife, The Chihuahua, is as unclear as her *Quinceañera's* dateline, one thing is sure: *they* invented love. If I can't find a *"folie à deux"* here, I'll stop my hankering.

The chaos of *Ze Goal Airport* creates the ambiance. I try my best at the customs:

"Euuh... Bonjour, je t'aime, je vois la vie en prose." I proudly said with a perfect Frawnch "R".

"Roh, encore ces Rosbifs! Pff!" The customs officer replied.

I won't let the grumpy man spoil my voyage.

I chose to visit the principal town called Love City, also known as the City of Lights or, as some might argue, the City of Lies.

First impressions might be correct. I love it all: the Lady of Steal, the crystal-clear blue Sapphire Scene River, the artistry, the high-end complaining, delicious crescent moons, and even carrier pigeons that seem better at delivering letters than the *Fed-Up* sparrows from Invictus Land.

Finally, the best of Frawn Land is undoubtedly its inhabitants, the delightful Frawnchies. They are one tricky species, adorable one minute, detestable the next. Maybe that's where that infamous doctor with a split disorder comes from.

***

We are getting interrupted by a brief argument. Seeing a couple breaking up on the Love-Lock Bridge – where people usually seal their bond for eternity – is incongruous. A North Port Prince heartbreaker trying to make it work after messing up always sounds like that guy in front of me: "Don't leave me, my dear. I love you under the sun, I love you in the rain. I'll love you forever and always" – maybe another poet.

While he's polishing his prose, I notice I can't feel my head, and my hands are red. Time is freezing along my nose and toes in the extreme cold.

Then, I received a call from my Frawnch friend Sam, the only one I kept from my international exchange student program. Guess who hasn't forgotten the fancy outing I promised him a year ago? Jules, Sam's son! *Dank*, he's welcome to join us.

I learn all my youngsters' slang from him. He says I'm "*Cheugy*", I hope it's positive!

Unfortunately, Jules is not interested in my plan to visit museums and castles. In the same way that hummingbirds are endlessly pecking in the Plane Tree Alley, Jules wants to eat, eat, eat – teenagers and their insatiable appetite.

We go to *La Claque*, The Bulldog's favorite restaurant, owned by Frawnch chef Juicy Smoothay. Should we try snails, frogs, or the fat liver? The latter doesn't sound good, but Sam tells me, "It's delicious, trust me."

Seconds later, eating again, macaroons. Minutes later, he asks for a second dessert: two white dunes with a sprinkle of cinnamon spice and served with an enjoyable molecular tea. Mrs. Whitersfork – the etiquette guru, would agree that connoisseurs should only taste this exquisite gourmet meal with a silver *spork* or a golden *knork*.

Welcome to the City of Love Handles.

***

My fattening frenzy is not important compared to the current news, though.

Remember the battle we were afraid had reached the point of no return in Holy Land? Well, one side wants "absolute winning." It means "game on," for better or mostly worse.

Who started, and who will repent first? They can't agree to disagree, so we should expect tremendous collateral damage.

Bad cop/bad cop, bad news...

***

No good news in the Xieta Verse to feel better?

NSL finale: from winning the Center Invictus poker division to winning the Invictus Land tournament, there was a round of applause for the 'Chefs' and the fantastic referees. I can't judge; I don't understand poker at all. The only thing I know is that Wild Valentine's team won!

Indeed, the Fountain City's 'Chefs' won a Super Masked Ball star for a second consecutive year. I heard Wild Valentine's teammate, Malone, will celebrate their win with his favorite food – fried chicken. Malone is one of the greatest in his category, so I might listen to his wife's advice and start eating more fried chicken to increase my gym performance – when I begin to exercise. They say anticipation is key!

Mrs. Invictana already knows that, so she enters the Super Masked Ball, so Cry School! She's not the cheerleader to the skater boy, but she's drinking with Rumor Girl and shimmering like we've never seen before. Philophiles can only be elated with the cherry on the cake, the chef's kiss, and the sweeter strawberries on their lips. I told you, here they are... inventing love all over again.

***

That poker stadium excitement echoes some Mother Land events.

Mother Land (+; –), the cradle of Motherans, is organized like Hope Union, meaning an aggregation of sovereign Lands. Mother Land is said to be the cradle of Xian life. Still, it faces multiple difficulties primarily because of its history of oppression from powerful Lands like Hope Union and Invictus Land. Besides, its challenges stem from current governance and development issues. Some would also point to Mother Land's lack of unity and strategy to better their lives.

In the meantime, like every Xian, Motherans use entertainment to escape their hardships. The yearly Drama Ball Cup is one good example of an event that brings joy to Motherans. The XX24 Cup takes place in western Mother Land and is hosted in Eyevory Land, the cradle of Eyevoryans, led by The Elephant.

After several twists, Eyevory Land's team wins XX24 Drama Ball Cup. How I learned about that? The Xieta Verse, still! It started with me trying to do the *shawala bam* shoulder dance, and I came across the hammer dance. As a dance enthusiast, I tried both and failed.

I didn't know you could make yourself cringe. Now, I do. If you don't, don't look for it; never try this at home. IYKYK.

***

Let the dancers dance; let the singers sing.

Hell yeah! Rush is XX24's headliner for the NSL after-Ball entertainment show. He starts the show with an all-blue royal suit. I get directly transported back in the day!

Rush let the poker stadium burn like he burned my hometown ballroom last year. Yes, I lost my voice that night, and I got it bad when the seizure dance started. As if I wasn't already struggling, S.H.E. brought her guitar and almost killed us; she is so talented. Is it me, or does she look like a famous nepo kid? At any rate, everybody ate.

That was even before Rush started ice skating, OMG! I can't keep up; it's something special.

A little confession: I'm just like the not-so-underdog Felicia who joined Rush on stage; I can't fall in love with my future boo because I *ain't* got time for that.

Fun fact: I could have been as good as Rush had I not turned down a contract in kindergarten. Yeah, I was that good with my *ABCs*! Sold out bathroom tour, guys! Listen to my mixtape or learn from my mistakes.

***

The Phoenix might be forced to learn a life lesson after an alleged court sentence linked to his gold company made the news. Let's see where that bracket goes.

***

Buzz.

The buzzing Virgo Queen, one of the world's best movie stars, officially enters XX24. Here we are, stirring up the hornets' nest.

Yee haw, she holds them! Her new movie project is a western.

Time has stopped, there's a cowboy showdown in the desert; she draws faster than her shadow, unsheathing her *Secrade* on her way to the saloon.

We will soon understand the outfit she was wearing at the last Granites. She arrived on a pink pony, wearing a rosé hat, giving me a good reason to raise my glass – sorry, my beer – to good ol' days.

Ya, she's a cowgirl now.

Her fans, known as the 'B-list defense lawyers' (or just B-list), would object and tell us she's always been one, born and raised.

* Louder for the people in the back! *

They might be right; Queen V was already there – just like Georgia, some days on our minds. Who's Georgia? We might never know.

I get a flashback from seeing Queen V with my own eyes being reborn last year for her movie premiere. She's just perfection – surreal. She's supposed to be older than me, but I feel 52, and she looks younger than 32. Maybe I should speed up the gym subscription process. I was drenched while sitting comfortably in an air-conditioned movie theater while she was matter than chalk on the premiere red carpet, and on screen.

Anyway, I am now connecting the dots; there was already a flying horse in her last movie. Her hair was glowing and flowing better than a Wowlywood actress. It felt like a Rokshi & Ranshi moment singing "*O crazy one.*"

A little confession: I missed a suitable moment to shut up during the screening. Like Jaze Steakham or the beekeeper Dave, I am ready for the B-list attack on that one. But some might understand, I just needed to say, "Hi Julio!" when he appeared as a walk-by extra in the film. He was my sports coach in college, and he's still fine, *fine*!

But I stray again.

One last thing: I can't stress enough how overjoyed I was seeing our dear Yellow for her first supporting role – the beautiful blossoming star. Like I said, I'm a very detached and objective fantasy journalist (*wink*). I can't wait to see what's next for the powerful mother-daughter duo.

***

I don't control my brain or my Xieta Verse feed, so please forgive me for thinking about this now.

I bet the MeTuber mom who tortured her kids may have wanted top lawyers to help her escape her fate. It won't be possible to get out and leave now.

This time, no excuses. *Fluff* apologies and crocodile tears.

I hope everybody's safe and happy now, virtual hugs.

***

It's show time on another scale. The opera singer Dame O'Purple just stepped down as commander of the night's watch – sorry, meal's watch. She confessed to using the magic potion of Oze.

I see the results on everybody; just be honest like her or say nothing. But if "the math ain't *mathing*," don't be surprised if you get some backslash.

You know what? I might give in, too, and apparently, some alternatives wouldn't affect the supply of people in actual need. But I still have that little voice telling me I can do it naturally.

Note to self: little voices should never be listened to.

***

On the love side, I'm the luckiest girl in the world. After an almost-dry February, I'm coming home with a Rush lookalike with a nice *rizz*; let's see where it goes.

I know we should never kiss strangers and tell. But I'm just ready to risk it all. I'm trying a lush life and the pursuit of happiness! Let's hope I won't end up homeless with a broken heart.

Lust at first sight; I blaze for him – *words*. I love to say: you light who you match.

Everybody likes to see Babe and me together. It *ain't* my fault. There's just that special something, an electric feel. We're calling it "love against all odds."

We're already talking about having kids. I wish I were joking!

Seely and her sentimental journey is the sweetest thing.

Let's call it a day!

In the meantime, here I am... still loving.

3

MARCH

HERE WE ARE... WORRYING.

Eves, Niamhs, and Fun Patricks' Month – let's gather to celebrate Us!

I am staying in my hometown in what used to be the first month of the year for some.

A wise little kid would say, "Seely's broke."

Luckily, Babe is a gentleman who doesn't split the bill on date night. He's taking me dancing at the Nuked King Night Club.

Just before The Ruler DJ starts, I order a few spicy margaritas. I already expect the next day hangover. Party girl lifestyle or nothing! I won't lie to you, I'm going down in my head, screaming "marry me Babe!"

The Ruler DJ plays all my favorite songs in his DJ set and brings the Doppelgänger dancers. I even forget I identify as a 52-year-old and jump all night long. I'm not ready for the aftermath at all, but that's the purpose of painkillers, I guess.

***

I have more battles on my fragile heart: the powerful Golden Eagle Land and its rival, Border Land. Unfortunately, they haven't found a resolution since they officially started fighting two years ago.

Border Land – also known as Underdog Land or U-Reign – is the cradle of Ureignans, led by The Killdeer. It's also considered a buffer frontier-Land between Hope Union and Golden Eagle Land.

Some people dispute The Killdeer's qualifications to rule, bearing in mind he's a former clown, and call into question his decision to fight his unbeatable enemy.

Most of Hope Union and the world seem on Border Land's side, and they keep pumping zillions into what they designate a "fight for freedom" as Ureignans and territories are facing a devastating toll.

This conflict has increasingly ostracized Golden Eagle Land, and it appears that the world couldn't care less. Maybe The Axolotl did, but somebody ripped the Goldian Red Moles' commander out of this sad world before he could confirm that. May his vessel fly higher than heaven.

As for The Libra – the current Golden Eagle Land leader, there's no doubt he's the only qualified person who can be trusted with Golden Eagle Land's gigantic power, so he is expected to rule forever. He's a vigorous man who exhibits a never-seen-before level of resilience. Even more so, an unknown enemy recently challenged his Land on its soil with a gruesome attack on a crowded event. Retaliations are expected.

For what it's worth, I am sorry for their losses and send prayers their way. As a compassionate Xian, all that tragedy hit me hard, and I can do nothing about it.

Is it my responsibility? No, it's just an example of a troubled soul's burden: stuck in a dizzy world, spiraling and feeling helpless.

***

Let's apply what I learned in Tales City, minding my beeswax. One solution might be to forgive and forget, escapism at its best.

Let's watch the Grit Awards from GB Land; it's worth it.

I see *you*, Slaye!

Let's also ackowledge a well-deserved lifetime award received by Rylie Nirogue, a fitting lollipop given to Sua Lima, a sleepwalking Kingslayer almost drowning on stage, a sugar-free venom given to a skydiving Connor, and a son of a Nun that is too busy earning an honest penny to show up.

For aye the same, psychopatic antics.

We can go back to body moving outside. I can take my life under control.

Sometimes, being delusional is as sweet as Italican ice cream and watermelon sugar. It's like booking another trip, 5-star hotels only, instead of investing your money or having enough savings if *fluff* hits the fan. Yes, there's a fine line between ambition and daydreaming.

***

Speaking of binball air line, the world's best binballer, The Brown, doesn't mind crossing the supersonic threshold.

Binball is similar to Earth's basketball, but it's played in the air, with players wearing solo-flying equipment. I learned from Xieta Verse sports news that The Brown has passed the bin barrier while flying at 40,000 feet. Sir, Planet X salutes you!

A little wink to Kate-Lynn on the ladies' side; she can do it, too – only 36,000 feet more to reach The Brown's level.

I could have achieved the same if I hadn't missed a step while descending the stairs on High School Prom Night. I tore my wrist and ankle, was rushed to the hospital, and missed my promised career and the love of my life, whom I was supposed to meet in the trophy hallway. It felt like I was cheated on by life.

I guess that's how the K-Anon society and The Phoenix fans felt when he didn't win the last *SYTYCR* five years ago. All is forgotten now.

People thought it was over for XX24 elections, but the Invictan One Big Court ruled The Phoenix was "free to go, *amigo*."

I'm not an expert in legal matters, but Invictan Big Three Court and One Big Court don't seem to agree on the same topic.

To Be Continued.

***

That's when Emmanuel, Cows, Beefs, The Dove, The Dromedary, and The Llama jump the fence and start to fight at Starstrucks due to a shortage of ingredients. Starstrucks is the dining hotspot in Deluwood. It is best known for the high-end culinary experience customers get thanks to its renowned celebrity Chefs. We all know the idiom about avoiding "too many cooks in the kitchen," right? Well, this is the perfect example.

It started with former athlete C. Gener going to Starstrucks, hoping to chit-chat with Lady Mama. To his surprise, C.Gener is told the now-vegan soul artist has changed her routine. Anyhow, he still wants Lady Mama's signature coffee drink, but the three chefs on site can't agree on the recipe.

Please concentrate on solving the math problem.

Chef The Dove likes three pumps of latte in his macchiato, but he can't find his milk frother.

The petty Chef The Llama doesn't need an extra pump of anything, but if C. Gener insists, he would instead add an extra shot of coffee, just one.

We don't know what the mumbling Chef The Dromadery's taste is yet, but he's allegedly keeping his head high and drinking extra virgin milk to avoid staining his apron.

We don't know who will win yet, but the dice are rolled. Everybody's talking about it, from the mayor to the neighbors with all their dogs.

✳✳✳

Better news: O'Stars night is on. As expected, Crees Nolo and Keylane Murf won for *Open-Namer.*

Emy Rock for *Rich Things* and Breyan Gooselind for *Dollbie.*

Isn't it ironic that Marlow Ruby, the main character of *Dollbie*, won nothing? Please don't ask my opinion; I haven't watched them yet. I was busy working and travelling, sorry.

***

More worrying news from my charming dwelling.

Her Grace The Kountess is nowhere to be seen. For someone who's not keen on playing hide and seek, real empaths should have known it was severe enough to back down. Please don't count on them.

I guess she then felt compelled to reappear in a way. She kept it simple and hit sent on a slightly edited family portrait. The madness got even worse to the point that people who swore the *Hypocrite Oath* did the unthinkable, trying to unveil her secret. The esteemed Kountess is now contrived to make a statement.

It's the Big K, scary.

I only wish for her, and all impacted to survive and thrive.

Keep your head up, kountesses, and do your best. We still need our crowns to shine bright like an almond diamond ring.

I know an Upper Feast Side Rumor Girl who should have saved an unintentionally hurtful joke or had better borrow one from her husband, Breyan Greynods. But that happens when you're immortal; what may have been funny 100 years ago is no longer.

I have a soft spot for her, though; she's just like me, misunderstood. We want to get rid of our split ends, have fun, wear our corals, drink ginger beer, and go to the movies. It's not a crime! We may even share big dreams and faded jeans if we must survive on a desert island one day.

Anyway, good luck, Big K babes!

I couldn't know yet that we would need luck more than ever this year. Anachronism is my guilty pleasure; they call it a casual rise and fall.

It's reminiscent of my 9 to 5 journey – just a wannabe working girl with a heart of gold, now forced to become an unknown legend.

***

I may be dreaming while reading stories about El Jefe, the King of *The Jungle*. I wouldn't have spent my burnt-out energy to write this manuscript if he hadn't believed in himself and started a jungle in his garage.

Having a garage is the common denominator of every success story, so I might ask my future husband or El Jefe's ex, Scozie, to help me get a fully equipped garage to be as successful. Why Scozie? She gives money faster than Dame O'Purple gives cars for free at the opera.

I'm telling you; the following check should have my name on it. Until then, I'll do a video tour of my place in case my future fans want a Chillflix documentary. If not, call me a lonely vlogger.

Maybe it's time to use Exron's brain-mic implant to ensure that what I manifest becomes reality.

Sorry for the confusion; Exron shared a video of his first guinea pig playing chess. It's a game I know I'll never understand or master without added superpowers. But I fear his technology might get me deeper into fantasy, a real-life *Richy Starichy*. For those who don't have the reference, it's one of Sack Apron's latest documentary projects.

Fun fact: I went to high school with Sack and heard he's now working for an NGO that promotes wellness and environmentally friendly initiatives. I'm unsure I understand everything, but I'm happy for him.

***

What most of the world doesn't seem to understand is ART; therefore I already know that my artistic project won't be understood or appreciated at its correct value. Luckily, I won't sell it to any Xian.

I feel for amateur artists, though, as I read somewhere that they shouldn't even ask for a Xi penny. Some people strongly disagree, and consider any price a bargain – especially for a historic cache.

It is, compared to almost a xillion spent by an art collector to buy the infamous floating door that saved a woman named Eve, and left her soulmate Adam behind. Remember one of those couples who invented love on a sinking ship? That was the start of Cathe and Lehoe's phenomenal ride after *they* survived, which is still unexpectedly going on 25 years later.

***

Speaking of art, there's a puppeteer artist's name that we can't keep out of our damn mouths.

Remember The Dandy? Let's introduce him properly. He's formerly known as Fluff Dandy, Fluffy, Uncle Lust, or The Dandler, as his nemesis named Sixty is calling him.

All roads lead back to Willi Winkatt and his predictions because Aliens are now invading The Dandy's house. Even Aliens were allegedly scared by what they saw at the puppeteer's mansion, the most concerning being tapes and baby oil. These Aliens couldn't proceed with the abductions because the floors were so oily that they slipped. *Ouch*

Aliens figured they needed to return to their dimension before their wormhole disappeared. They took some photos and made a List of a dark web of culprits. We're waiting for their return on Planet X to know if people we are now side-eying should be side-eyed.

I need something stronger than wine for that one. I can try a spicy Mermaid-on-the-rocks cocktail, but I'm not a certified barista – it might taste like a Wowlywood dish.

One day, I might receive my mixology accolade like Kenny Hard did this year. The famous Invictan mixologist added a March Twin award under his feet so he could finally reach the top of his shelf to grab the liquor.

***

Let's exit this month with a colorful bang!

Forget about Wowlywood stars like Charook, Allintab, Amor, Hushwaya or Priceyankee. Meet Rhanan and Adakhi AllBeaming, the new main characters of Golden Sparrow Land. They invented love right before arriving on an elephant's back. We adore a Wowlywood cliché.

Expect astonishing festivities for their engagement. You read that correctly; it's not the wedding yet.

Everybody's included: Mr Zu Burger, tradwife pioneer Aimee and family, and the now-good gyal, Robean.

Stop everything you were doing, including reading this, and watch what's happening: a live painting event.

Robean, the Triangulum Islands' Queen, is a world-renowned painter and street artist. She has left her artistry to start new ventures, leaving her fans in complete disarray.

Robean chose an emerald dress reminiscent of her native translucent waters. We don't know if it's Wowlywood-inspired, but we love it. We're good if she's happy and closer to a lip gloss painting than a retirement plan.

With this event, she gives her fans a little hope that she might get back on track. The new painting we've all been waiting for might be released sooner than later. Not that night, she's just reproducing one of her famous 45 seconds art. It's better than nothing.

Thank you, AllBeaming family!

Have you ever experienced a déjà vu episode? I just did. Unless I'm crazy, it looks exactly like another AllBeaming engagement party. It wasn't Robean then, but Queen V, who did an exclusive private movie premiere there a few years ago.

***

Speaking of the latter, it's the moment to have the complete vision board for the Western movie, including the horse-riding act. Whether or not the other cowboys like it, she's now on Invictus' Wild West Side. She was born to be popular, an eternal sunshine who can't be confined to ordinary things.

It's not her first rodeo. I heard she worked her whole life to build the cinema empire she now has. Logical, I believe a diva is nobody's soldier. Queen V unapologetically commands and rules her life. But I think one can only reach this level of success under certain conditions: a great imagination, extreme dedication, and choosing the hard stuff like starving and exercising – over sleeping and crying *me mom* a river. I could make the same choices and happily jump out of bed when I hear my alarm clock. But all I *wanna* do is have some fun, be myself, and soak up the sun.

I don't know why my little voice is still trying to convince me it's not too late to start something new.

I'm feeling stuck in my life while writing those sweet words in my little room, staring at the wall. I'm alone with my thoughts all this time, dreaming of a lottery win and a paradisiac life.

"Beware of darkness," my mother would say.

If it makes me happy, it can't be that sad, right? I'm incredibly ok; seeing the positive in life is my number one priority. I'm just waiting for a twist of fate, but the universe is radio silent. Time won't wait, so I guess I should take my doctor's advice and freeze my eggs.

In the meantime, here I am... still worrying.

4

APRIL

H ERE WE ARE... HURTING.

It's time for independence days and Planet Earth's Month!

Wear your green and your shamrocks to protect yourself from bad luck!

I'm pregnant!

I promise it's not a foolish April's joke or an Esther egg; I'm pregnant!

I get worried when I hear gurgling noises; I don't know how I will survive an actual Xian being growing inside of me.

Lo and behold, I know the creepy tiny creature will make a smashing entry!

Ditzy Seely is going to have an itsy-bitsy her, it's so bizarre. I can't believe it!

No, I'm not pregnant, but Enshanti is! A table for three, Baby!

I'm so happy for her and her husband, Naily.

You heard me right; I said husband, not baby daddy.

Forget about the rest; they are always on time for Love!

Was Lady Clover invited to the wedding? No, she wasn't. But she doesn't mind, she just loves happy endings!

I'm not a hopeless romantic, but even I can admit their rekindle is *rekindling*.

Now, I want it that way or the highway. I also want to travel. My right brain can only listen to my bank account manager for one month. We all witnessed what staying home did to my mental health last month. Let's whoop it up and find ourselves a wonderful scenery.

***

Scientists say that we all descend from Mother Land. There's no debate here – this is my fantasy. I make the rules, and they perfectly fit the narrative.

I happen to understand the calling I received. I'm going back home.

Doesn't it feel good to book a trip?

Here I come, Gifted Land, the cradle of Egiftans, led by The Seahorse.

Let's navigate this month along the Happy River, the father of Mother Land's rivers.

We all just hope we won't have to solve any murder mystery on our way...

It's hot in here, but the poetry of the landscape is difficult to miss.

I have stars in my eyes. The Happy River flows in me slowly; I'm chained to the rhythm of cymbals, flutes, lyres, and harps. I'm wide awake, but my heart is chasing tornadoes. Like the whirlers, I'm levitating and spinning away to reach the ascent.

It looks so perfect until dizziness and vertigo kick in.

I'm back to reality; we enjoy a lovely Cosharing tea to end the night. You know you're getting old when you start eating and drinking things because of its beneficial properties. That's why I didn't say no to a bit of honey in my hot tea.

I overheard the server's manager suggesting he should have waited for the tea to cool down to add the natural and nutritious sweetener. I immediately take the server's defense. He's professional, young and beautiful. Who cares?

I don't even like honey, hot or cold – except the beekeeper Dave's *Lucky Stuff*. It always finds its way into my mouth – as if the victorious 50-year-old spicy nectar had a mind of its own, so mysterious.

***

Daylight in Gifted Land, let's put our explorer outfit on and enjoy the treasure hunt. There's something special about being present in a monument built in a long gone past, hoping for better future days.

I can't wrap my head around the fact that there are so many misunderstood scribbles in Gifted Land's ancient ruins. In this day and age, it becomes clear that no one should take the risk of having our common heritage wiped out because people didn't take the time to write their stories, re-count crucial events and ensure the code to decipher our words remain available to infinity and beyond.

We can find another proof that writing and art are as old as the beginning of our existence in the recent discovery of a narrative cave art in East Wind Land (+; –) depicting people hurting a pig. It also shows that hate and cruelty are as old as Planet X.

So many people live without being bothered by all this negativity, but I can't.

Maybe I'm a time traveler stuck in another dimension behind a library where this repository sits. No one truly understands me, just like the meaning of a spinning top.

That's the beauty of it: few have the gift of prophecy. To the ones who do, please let us know when we'll finally reach the peace and love era worldwide.

By adding a little perspective on our common Mother Land origin, we shouldn't fight about anything. Indeed, we all come from the same place. Still, it remains important to note that we parted ways xillions of years ago. Otherwise, we would be a big inbred Targorion family – my biggest fear. It's not my cup of tea; like I told you, I chose the brain.

***

Sorry to be redundant. While visiting museums and wonders of the ancient world, I hear that Holy Land conflicts are ongoing and neu-tral, helpful parties become collateral damage. What a pity; I wish I or anyone could have the right words to make it stop for good.

Some are condemning, others are defending. Everybody should unwind and, if not supportive, keep their nose out of it. Or they could follow the People of Calm Morning Land (+; −) and use their vote to express their opinions.

It would still be necessary for every Land to have elections on everything that could impact them.

***

I promised I would try the good news/bad news thing; let's all concentrate on Beachella!

We love a beach volleyball festival, tongs, tans, and an Apple Fizz cocktail. The "who's who" of "shake that" is there! Who's that? Among the headliners for the after-game event, you have The Whiteners, Nice Rice, Korat Cat, Lanigator del Sun, Styler the Inventor, Dobrina Esprenter, Tygrer, Crimes, Legal, and Victa Money.

It sounds like a lot of fun, and there is no doubt that Mrs. Invictana and her Wild Valentine, who joined the festivities, enjoyed their well-deserved break. Look at them in matching magic hats, inventing love, still.

They can afford it, as *Forge Brochure* just revealed that Mrs. Invictana is now a Zillionaire, among the luckiest; welcome to the Z club! But considering that *Forge Brochure* doesn't have VIP-tent access to her financials, let's allege all that. Receiving the news this month may also be an April fool's prank, so let's not jump to conclusions and blindly believe everything.

Speaking of jumping, Smarties can't wait to resume the happy earthquakes. In the meantime, they finally have a dragon egg explosion from Mrs. Invictana. The newly acclaimed poet just released her manuscript, revealing the new play.

So, what do we think about the *PTSD* of the Alive Poets Society's spokesperson?

Deep.

It's deep.

Timing is also crucial here. It may be about love, but I make it about loss.

Just like Bobby Rain Dear, I might only understand 15% of it, but let's call a spade a spade; it's a masterpiece, a record-breaking one.

Conspiracy challengers would even try to find a link between the damsel in distress' PTSD theme and the year of the Dragon. Let's add a Gorilla fight in the mix, and we might create an April Fool's circus.

Anyway, I digress and can't help but parallel the discovery of Pathos' carbonized scroll.

How did his life end? Well, one of the greatest philosophers that ever lived wasn't too happy about the music being played on his deathbed and criticized the musician's "scant sense of rhythm." Some might see the irony of Pathos writing that comment on his last days, knowing that the late philosopher considered music one of the least prestigious good things. Others would argue that if he pointed out the danger music could pose, he still thought it important enough to help the youth's education and reach social harmony.

***

I couldn't keep any secret from you, so you already know how down bad I felt in March. Now, even an enjoyable trip can't enliven me.

Kismet stroke closer to home, and after a brave battle, we unfortunately lost a beautiful angel – The Best, gone too soon to share her philosophy of happiness.

Saying goodbye to a loved one opens a cut that always bleeds and never heals. Everybody is stoic and putting on a brave face, so I'm left to keep a stiff upper lip.

I don't want to be a killjoy; it's just the way I'm feeling. Memories become a curse and a blessing – hanging on to them not to forget but avoiding them not to suffer. Hoping to meet again in a found heaven is the only consolation.

We haven't gone through the whole year yet, but *The Fate I Can't Escape* is repeatedly playing on TV.

Feeling a kind of hurt that no words or tears can translate. I can't help but wonder, "Who's next?"

Happy stuff, right? Well, let's find comfort in sound or book a trip.

My money, my rules. We only live once.

***

Sometimes, essential news allows us to get back to reality and re-connect to what matters. I don't know if what follows does, but if you were wondering, The Phoenix is not backing down.

He's one of a kind, now trying to defend himself on a new case. Old familiar tune... to be defined.

***

Remember the fight at Starstrucks? If you don't, that's a You problem. The rest of us are moving on.

The Dove – the most peaceful Chef, who was expected to do a live cooking show in Angels City, flies low on his private supersonic plane, then does a touch-and-go on the runway, aborting his landing. He wasn't too sure about it – better be safe than sorry, right?

The Dove doesn't need those three pumps of latte anymore; he's willing to give his drink to whoever wants. He took The Deer's high road and flew away.

Why am I shedding a tear?

Because I would have liked the other two to do the same.

Na, I'm lying like the sodium pundit. The beef slice is too delicious to say *No*. Sorry, I'm drifting. As you can see, I'm still struggling to follow my diet plan.

Unlike me, The Dromedary is hitting the gym, feeling stronger after doing push-ups, and he finds his voice back. My ADHD brain is now wondering who had stolen it and who had Robean's money.

The Dromedary continues to run on the treadmill and the hamster wheel, using unorthodox methods to get his point across.

The comeback is good, but the copycat technology and name-dropping (Mrs. Invictana's maid, among others) might receive backlash.

Before he can continue with the rower machine, The Llama strikes back with an innovative 6-minute microwave dish.

All that happens while The Dove remains absent: "Please leave him a message."

***

We just reached the end of the Happy River cruise, and I feel tortured about leaving. I don't like goodbyes. The worst are the never-ending ones that start in the living room, continue by the door, and end in the car. Who's leaving at the end? We don't even know anymore.

What I know is that I enjoyed Mother Land and Motherans.

I also checked a few things in my not-written-yet bucket list: flying in a hot-air balloon despite my acrophobia, camel riding in the desert despite my erimophobia, visiting magnificent colored tombs despite my coimetrophobia, going inside a pyramid despite my claustrophobia, trust a local driver despite my amaxophobia and taste local treats in the market despite my self-diagnosed gluten intolerance. Done.

I might sound cliché, but the connection with locals was the most amazing and memorable thing about this trip. They seem to be happier with less. How can I complain even one day when what I have is considered more? To each their own. Let's fake it till we make it.

In the meantime, here I am... still hurting.

5

HERE WE ARE... ENJOYING.

Planet X's Laughter Month!

It was an intense trip. I feel more spiritual and connected to my long-lost roots.

Let's hope you won't see me around kissing trees with the *Meet & Greed Gala* people.

The *Meet & Greed Gala* is an invite-only imagination contest created by Zina Zintour. The year's theme is 'Pretty in Coma City: Resuscitating Compassion.'

Too bad Rumor Girl didn't show up; that's her lane; comedy might not be. Luckily, people in attendance upped their game; they are so creative and elegant.

Let's comment on the looks.

Zeneia is giving us a floral and frugal death stare.

The mermaid Serene Willing is giving homage to the O'Stars' golden statue, a metaphor of life or death legacy that simple minds missed – or maybe she missed the theme.

Lanigator del Sun is fabulous in her attire – the apparent metaphor of night angst caused by invisible but noisy mosquitoes.

G-Jean can't make a faux pas when perfectly depicting a fragile blooming white rose.

The charming Tygrer is making her entrance with the most anxious clutch of all, an hourglass. Taking our breath away, literally, thinking about time, the most precious thing we all share – yet the scariest as no one ever caught it. Tygrer might be the first to succeed, considering her one-of-a-kind persuasion skills. Here she is, being held like a mannequin. She's a Tygrer girl in a Tygrer world. Give her the keys to Deluwood already!

There were more people, but I am still running out of time – only a few days left to finish this...

But that doesn't mean I can't find ourselves a lovely scenery.

***

I introduce you to my beloved North Port Land, part of Hope Union, the cradle of Northportese led by The Marmoset. Let's go to my home away from home – Unbeaten City; I'm back!

"Bom dia."

"Olá."

"Como vai?"

"É bom e você?"

"Está indo muito bem obrigada."

Upon arrival, I am reminded that this city has one of the most beautiful supersonic-train stations I've seen. Its walls are beautifully decorated with frescos of tiles depicting daunting stories: battles, conquests, farming, and festivities.

I can hear the imaginary workers who built this twelve years ago while singing, "Mrs. Invictana & the North Port Prince (*alright*), we're so mad, we tiled the plane blue, the soon-to-be elected unlikely to fly away... with you."

I will seek therapy at some point, I promise.

Tourists are mesmerized, taking a thousand photos and videos they'll never return to, blocking the locals from catching their trains. Yes, it seems like real people live here, have jobs to get to, kids to drop off at school, and dinner parties to attend. Who would have thought? I'm living my best life: as always, the food is good, the sun is shining, the wine is *wining*. There are so many wineries; WOW! I may have some red wine problems, but I am functioning, smiling, and partying!

Now that I'm traveling more, I look at this city where I spent part of my childhood in a new light.

There are a lot of places I haven't had the chance to visit and a lot of things I haven't experienced, so let me be a proper tourist, too.

I want to do everything: the blue stadium, the black cape singing, the orange rooftop views, the river and its famous bridges.

***

Work hard, play harder.

Well, I know a player who should have tried to work on our relationship instead of swinging from branch to branch like a wild lemur. Babe abandoned a powerful tree to rest on a weak limb. That small man said he would never leave me, but I was wrong; people change. Long story short, Babe Frawnch-exited my life and disappeared like Houdini.

Maybe that's my avoidant attachment disorder striking again, but to me, it's not worth the fight. Right guy, wrong time, or just good riddance. Run! Next! I forgive him, though; big girls don't cry; they watch crime series and dress for drama.

In any case, trying to connect with people when you're not connected to yourself might always fail.

Strangely, I still think that the best is yet to come. I'm alive, and I won't stop trying. I talked to a friend about my trips, and he agreed that making a wish to the genie at a Brothay show was silly. He told me I needed to go to a FAbulous, TImeless, and MAjestic place if I wanted the real deal. I followed his advice and ended up in the nearby City of Miracles. I followed people around and lighted a candle.

The coin is flipped; let's see how it goes.

***

I hope better than Tim Broady's birthday roast on Chillflix TV.

I have always wondered why anyone who can afford the best restaurants would agree to be served unseasoned biddy. I might never know the answer. They say it's for the show, just like the spicy hot-dogs eating game.

The "who's who" of "play that" is at the table! Aimee – the tradwife pioneer – is there and getting more booed than a mean pariah, and she's ordering a seemingly delicious hummus.

Luckily, the famous barista Kenny Hard is spitting better bars than cooks and bringing his short drinks – sorry, shot – sponsored by *La Niña Caramina* to make everyone forget the disaster meal.

Thanks to the great waiter, Vicki Glacier, I can identify the rest of the attendees who are unfamiliar to me.

We have Broccoli Man, a great guy with a bright smile and a teddy bear's heart. He's known for being the only Xian with a body composed of 90% water and 10% CTV. At least, he didn't fall into the pre-Xi market crash's trap caused by BankruptMan's company, as Tim Broady did in XX21. As soon as Broccoli Man is free, I'll marry him!

One of Oze's magicians was also invited, but I didn't catch his name – almost irrelevant. Vicki considers him a sleb, though.

If memory serves me right, Tim Broady is a poker master of the NSL who broke NSL records with Ball Chicbelly. It's not easy to recognize him without his poker sunglasses.

Tim Broady is also the Lord of Paper Rings, G-Zen's nice-looking former husband.

They were a perfect-looking couple! I don't know what happened, and I choose to keep off until my inner conversation kicks in.

"No?!"

"Really?"

"She did what?"

"Because he didn't want to retire?"

"I've always known martial arts were dangerous."

Well, that's something else I don't understand. I'm getting out of my shell for the first time in my life because I need to find another solution than decades with imposture syndrome. I don't think I'll ever feel that kind of passion, one that would make me sacrifice a hot, tall man.

***

Maybe I'm overthinking it. Maybe not, because I've seen this kind of passion more than once.

The popular ventriloquist Matryoshka is one good example. She threw the biggest get-together in Barrio Land (–; –) to celebrate her achievements. She closed her goodbye tour with force. The unquantifiable crowd at the beach and in the streets now live to tell how impressive the best night of their lives was.

Like it or not, there's only one Matryoshka, and she's not ready to hang up the show. She's one of a kind, beautiful inside out, an unapologetic icon. That's what I admire about her. She might not be in today's ventriloquist charts, but she has nothing to prove to anyone – "been there, done that." Again, if you know Matryoshka, you know.

My apparent personality couldn't be more opposite to hers, but to be honest, I am a rebel at heart. I'm just not bold enough to act on my thoughts, start a revolution, or become a trendsetter.

I'm a good follower, though; a win is a win. "W."

That's why I love hearing about daring new princesses and queens being crowned every year. I agree that they all deserve fitted gowns and shiny crowns. Kings and princes do, too; everybody's included.

If you didn't get the code for the memo, choose any letter in the alphabet; it will open the repository.

Love makes every planet rotate, whether it's flat or round.

***

Maybe that's why a representative from Red Dragon Land decided to visit Love City, too. I hope he enjoys it even better than I did and will try the new bread-scented post-stamp.

***

On the representative side, there is little news from The Phoenix.

He's in court again regarding some whispering bills. One of his anonymous accusers, H.D., is confronting him face-to-face. But we already know him. He wasn't born a quitter, just like his BFF from Golden Eagle Land.

Indeed, The Libra is throwing a big party to celebrate his winning. He's ready for another term, still on his own terms. His Land, his rules. That should be respected: *su casa no es tu casa*. Don't bring María to the *carne asada*, or you'll end up with an unwanted permanent residency.

But the event wasn't as successful as Matryoshka's; his fellow leaders didn't RSVP because of irreconcilable differences, and I find it rude. If I get emotional about a kid's birthday being ruined because no one showed up, I feel the same way in this situation.

Also, communication should never stop because that's how a good villain story starts, and no one wants that. When you corner someone, they might feel like there's no option but to fight for their own survival and may end up doing something you wouldn't expect from them.

I know what I'm talking about.

That's me projecting. Luckily, The Libra couldn't care less, just like Talers.

Speaking of, Tales City now has the most xillionaires in the world. When successful people get that *Tales'* best-seller status, we all know where they're heading.

***

I'm believing in myself a little more every day. I've been jet-lagged about being strong-willed, but I now realize I've always been ahead of my time. I never quit. Just like 'That Girl' Mary – the famous Xian rights activist, I just prioritized my mental health.

It wasn't talked about much back then, and even now, I am pretty sure that my family or my close circle of imaginary friends wouldn't believe me if I told them I was struggling.

Their reaction would be:

"HAHA, that's the best one you did this year.

Like the timing and the delivery.

Haha.

Struggling?!

Hehe."

It's comforting to see people with more to lose than me being vocal about how they feel. Whether you're a pageant winner or a pro-level athlete, representation is representation, and I know it's helpful to many.

***

About speaking up, I know some meddlers are only here for the fight at Starstrucks.

What's new?

The Llama now adds oil to the fire with a public statement: The Dromedary is "Just like them." Who's them? Like my purpose in life, we don't know yet. What we know is that he's willing to pay ₰6.16 for his extra shot of coffee, not a penny more, not a penny less.

The Dromedary is now trapped in the corner, not in the closet.

He gets his lips and claws out, and almost rips The Llama's heart with relationships and family affairs allegations. But because he's too big and Starstrucks is too crowded, he does collateral damage.

AceApp, Robean's hubby, is among the victim of a random scratch. The couple invented love in a hopeful place, and they're busy being Zillionaires, making 100 kids, and having no paint release.

On top of that, AceApp is allegedly in a muddy situation after pleading the second and the fifth during a heated argument. While he's enjoying precious family time, one would understand that The Dromedary is irrelevant to them. Sorry, not sorry.

The Llama now stoops to The Dromedary's level and investigates his baby's status. Before waiting for a response, The Llama drops another smile; the chart is charting; the coffee is 100° hot!

The Dromedary's 3-pumps-of-latte drink is getting cold, and The Llama releases a public service advice to use it with caution, citing "a drink that any celiac person should stay away from to avoid an allergic reaction, especially if you're a minor."

Public Health officials are yet to confirm the concern.

***

While we're waiting for their return, The Dandy saga continues... His former lover, the beautiful and talented Classy Cherry, spoke up against him. With receipts released, there are no unfounded doubt, and stupid victim blaming anymore – it's about time.

They say where there's smoke, there's fire. Everything seemed to burn down like hell in front of us, but nobody could see it, or everybody had their eyes closed.

To prevent that from happening again in the future, maybe there's a new technology that Exron or Zu Burger can develop so that we can spot invisible fires faster. I heard that BlackJag, an up-and-coming tech competitor, is testing a beta product. Haters will say that it has no value, and it's just smoke and mirrors like BankruptMan's company. There is no shade at the latter, but he should have kept his poor advice to invest in the cryptic money.

I guess the future will tell us who was right and who was left, whether we are ready or not. Let's hope that no misunderstanding or miseducation will be allowed. Because nothing else matters anymore except the truth. I bet anyone would agree to light a candle for that one.

***

Anyway, I'm a lost cause. I promised to live in the moment, so let's just unread the room. Can we please have fun now?

Let's lose control and throw a lavish Regency-themed party for my last night in Unbeaten City!

The place is beautifully decorated with floral arrangements, royal decor, and vivid colors. It's magnificent; I stepped into another era.

My fellow Ladies and Lords are here, and the drinks are flowing.

It's always fun around Lady Tootle Dawn and the gorgeous Ms. Luiguine Lope. I can't say the same when I cross by the haughty Lady Cooling Fridgerstone, Miss Daf Naynay, Ms. Charming, Lady Fregate, Mr. Hurry, Lord Ray, or Lord File.

Forgive me, I almost forgot to do a cringe, exaggerated curtsy to my good Lord Chairman and Her Monarch Queen Chariot.

We talk about secrets, plots, rivalries, but mostly about love.

We found ourselves in rather rare agreement that *Amore* deserved the Olive Branch prize at the Sugar Cane Festival in Frawn Land this year.

Also, 'That Girl' Mary is among laudable ladies who won a distinction for their outstanding documentary, *Cornelia Priest*, promoting Xian rights defense. I haven't watched it yet, but my fellow ladies consider the prize much deserved. They say it's revolutionary and may help protect those in need, work for fair justice worldwide, and spark a change.

Then, we debated the concept of a participation trophy, but we had to leave before reaching a consensus. We promised to catch up and organize an afternoon tea soon.

In the meantime, here I am... still enjoying.

6

JUNE

HERE WE ARE... PARTYING.

June Baby! Cheers to the Month of Youth and Pride!

Hangover is not a good way to start the month.

What a night!

I got so drunk that I took the mic to sing my favorite bar song. My one-night fling offered drinks, and everybody went on the dancefloor. We did everything from line dancing to dropping it low and whining; it felt like a night from the past, from the IXs. I might not be the only nostalgic party animal who thinks everything was better before. We are the last of our kind because today's soirées look more like a book club than a night club. As Jules would say, "L." Everybody's sitting, not even looking at each other, and taking photos to show off the fun they're not actually experiencing.

It's just as dull as my job that doesn't even get me enough money to travel *and* afford a bottle of *Copper Spade* sparkling wine, *Lord Davi's, 313, Aerospace, La Niña Caramina*, or even *Mineral* water. Not only that, but in my old age, I'm still window shopping and unable to pay for my *Flannel* or *Harness* bag.

I can still make a little trip here and there; let's cross the sea and find a satisfactory scenery.

***

After a trip abroad, it only takes me one hour to return to my natural apologizing to everyone for everything.

From time to time, I must leave my cute Polite Village to go to Great Banter Land's biggest megalopolis, Big Smoke City.

Good day, it is raining; the sky is grey, and I wouldn't have it any other way. I am exceedingly delighted to be amongst well-mannered peers.

Like 16 xillion locals, a passing double-decker coach splashed me.

I apologize; I must have been on the wrong side of the pavement.

I want to pay the fine, but the coach driver insists it's his fault. I beg to cover the cost of my defective spatial awareness. Then, a very courteous and chuffed coach passenger interrupts us with a lovely interjection: "Carry on, bruv! I haven't got all day mates."

The knackered chauffeur finally accepts my offer, and we go on with our respective days.

So thrilled to be home.

***

While enjoying tea by the Eyesis River's big wheel, I read about a humorous event: a bat experienced love at first sight for a dark magic performer, The Pretty Heedless. Blinded by its attraction, that bat clung to her for dear life. She didn't even fling. What a bat-arse lady!

Let's hope this encounter doesn't start a mysterious pandemic. We already have a few set off by lovely Motherans who can't leave these creatures alone, putting Planet X at risk. That's what happens when you battle hunger. Still, better bats than Xians.

Anyway, The Pretty Heedless survived. Heaven knows that brush would have made me want to die on a hill house. Yet, before that thought crossed my mind, my chiroptophobia would have probably sent me faster to hell's kitchen or made me jump higher than the gloating Golden Girl.

Notwithstanding, no one can compete with The Golden Girl.

We all know women are masters at multitasking, but The Golden Girl's ability to balance her blissful life should be studied.

In the past year, she won a ninth circus acrobatics title in Invictus Land and still had time to put her husband (or love co-inventor) on the map. Alrighty, I am just plugging his leg; we all knew who he wasn't before meeting her. Unnoticeable, just like his fellow professional poker player, Wild Valentine, before he sent his Cupid arrow to Mrs. Invictana.

I concur with their admirers that the tenacious men made no mistake when courting their ladies.

***

Speaking of, while visiting the Great Bell after a mass, I overheard Mrs. Invictana had just arrived in Big Smoke City for her theatrical spectacle. The whole GB Land is now all hers, and we know a Smartie tsunami is incoming.

Now I understand the unusual happiness displayed by the Grits; it's her!

I'm as lost as a tourist in Big Smoke City, so I asked my way to a Smartie and ended up with 13 happy bracelets. The happy jewelry is embossed with a code to decipher. I'm not as bright as them; I still haven't found their meaning.

An ultra Smartie appeared out of nowhere and whispered to me: "The blue bracelet's code will give you the location of the beginnings' guardian, and the green one will open the Recognition's vault." Whatever that means... I'm okay, as long as this is not some voodoo spell.

On my way to meet the horse guards, I bumped into many Smarties, and when I arrived, I realized I was covered in glitter. Dazzled by the happy sparkles, I did the unthinkable: I touched the horse's reigns. I ask for forgiveness; I reckon getting bitten and kicked by the horse is a fair punishment. Funny enough, Smarties around knew better; they were shaking their heads and telling me I was on my own in this mess. How supportive of them!

While trying to hide in shame, I noticed one girl lying on the floor, seemingly in distress, so I rushed to rescue her. I was ready to do CPR on her as Dr. Like taught me, "Chest compressions, Chest compressions, Chest Compressions," but I figured she could breathe. She's alive, phew, what a relief! She was just laughing uncontrollably.

Her name is Ellie, and she's a pure Invictan go-getter breed. Even Jane Gardener – the Chief of the Ancestors' Police – would agree.

Ellie and I couldn't be more different, but we got on well and bonded over that silly moment. She introduced me to Smarties circus and tried explaining the meaning behind the multitude of twinkling outfits passing by. Hippies and pixies wearing camel, tartan and pink.

I went along with her in front of the merch truck to get "the tote bag completing her collection." I didn't ask for it, but she gave me one, too. We may have found ourselves a xillionaire friend because that provision bag is not cheap. Still more reasonable than the lingerie.

I paused and realized I discovered that word for the first time: merch. I have never been a fan of anyone (except for my parents, if they end up reading this), so I never wore merchandise. I wonder how the merch meetings go like:

"I want as many of my head as possible. Try and capture my aura for each play."

"Here it is. It slaps, periodt!"

"NICE, gorgeous!"

Ellie – my newfound Smartie bestie – told me she traveled all the way from Invictus Land and was supposed to go to Mrs. Invictana's spectacle with her boyfriend the next day, but he broke up with her at the airport. Apparently, she has chosen laughter over dark thoughts, and she has "no tears left for him."

Ellie then invited me to join her for the show as a thank-you gift for trying to save her unthreatened life.

I agreed, convinced she would text me to retract her invitation, as I have already experienced so many times. She didn't.

A little confession: as an introvert, there was also a risk that I would not feel like leaving my hotel the next day.

Anyway, I said yes.

Smarties' honor is respected, and here we are... inside a gigantic theatre arena, unexpectedly at a Smartie party.

As usual, I'm talking to myself: "Lady Seely Clown, welcome to *The Auras* tour."

Great Banter Land doesn't disappoint; it's raining, so I guessed organizers would have canceled everything.

There is no cancellation with that one. It's on!

Mrs. Invictana is the rainmaker; she can't fear a deluge.

The first narrators start with the theatrical troupe, Por Amor, with their lead drama actress, Haili. I don't understand the minority of Smarties in the house who are not concentrated for the opening act right now. Haili is epic, with powerful words, delivery, and an extraordinary aura. I'm just wondering if she's Xian because I'm freezing despite being wrapped up, and she's wearing a very light attire with no concern on her face. Maybe somebody stole her usual blue dress before she entered the stage.

Anyway, I'm blown away. Haili makes her outro, and the excitement is getting out of hand.

We all know what's coming next.

Ellie is as excited as if it wasn't the 100th play she was attending.

Despite the wind peaking up, the curtain-up starts.

The giant iridescent seashell prop slowly opens, and the main character makes her stage entrance, glistening like a pearl.

Here she is – the legendary Mrs. Invictana.

The decibels are reaching dangerous levels. I fear I might lose my hearing sense; I wasn't ready for it.

I am speechless.

Joy.

Love.

Respect.

Why am I getting emotional? Maybe because I received dreadful news right after I agreed to come to the show with Ellie. I didn't want to be the second person to stand her up, so I showed up – one of the best decisions of my life. Instead of brooding silently and getting to a dark place, I'm surrounded by joy, love, and respect.

I might not reach the same level of happiness as real Smarties, but it's a start.

Yes, my middle school classmate came a long way. From heartbreaks and broken things to the endgame, she's still the strong and undefeated Mrs. Invictana.

We never know how life will surprise us, but we might be a few decisions away from finally being best friends.

No, we're not.

She already has 22 besties, and I am antisocial.

Now that ship has sailed somewhere over the rainbow seas, let's hope she won't hate me because I'm allergic to hate, and I'm way too young to die dead. I need at least to tell my All-Time Crush, "We invented Love," before I join the long-gone shimmering stars and galaxies in the sky.

Mercifully, she doesn't know I exist and will never.

Back to *The Auras.* My scientific brain is trying to understand how every technical aspect of the theatre play works while my creative brain is soaking it up. She's delivering a perfect act and makes it look easy in *fluffing* stilettos.

I can't return the compliment to Smarties shouting the script next to me, but who am I to judge? I can't even remember my work passwords after a week's holiday, so hats off to them for their infinite memory.

"Speaking of hat, isn't it?" I ask Ellie.

"No, it can't be." She interrupted, while shaking her head.

"Bet!" I shouted.

"Oh yes, it is... Wild Valentine on stage!" She shouted back in total disbelief, with her hands on her head.

The whole theatre is losing their minds. Wild Valentine on stage to give her a *Boo'hoo'o'wa'er!*

Mrs. Invictana is blushing, rehydrated, and finding her motivation to finish her performance.

The winsome couple had a hard launch with His Grace The Kount's family. Now, this is something new. Smarties wanted to see unhinged behavior, so she gave it to them.

Speaking of His Grace, thankfully, his beloved wife – Her Grace The Kountess – is recovering and progressing well. She will soon make an appearance full of colors for the troops. I love the good news!

Back to colors, I got 31 more multicolored happy bracelets representing all the drama play's acts and scenes.

I guess it's not written "theatre newcomer" on my forehead, as many Smarties ask me my favorite act. I don't know, unfortunately; I'm not good at picking. I like all of them for different reasons.

No one should ask me to choose; I always say something stupid. At least not as ridiculous as the great improvisational theatre actor Dane

Growl. The older man made a silly joke during his improv, but the landing failed.

Why do all these non-certified humorists decide to imitate Gabe Churchelle? That's *his* lane, "Back off, everybody, me included!"

So, I was saying I'm as undecided as a metronome to pick a side. Still, if Ellie's unscathed life depended on it, the silly game would become: "Kiss Burgundy Street's Stalker, Marry Lord Everlore, Cheat Middays, Kill the fearful Tailor-made Suit's guardian for the money *sorry celestial God*, Have PTSD, Hire XX89 lawyers and Tell the Recognition jailor Now."

Paramount information: Just between you and me, I still haven't watched a full play, mainly because of my inattentiveness issues. But we'll get there someday, I promise.

A little rewind is necessary; Wild Valentine was on stage.

Everything about their relationship is so romantic. I don't want to seem like an envious brat, but why can't I have the same? I'm doing everything right! I don't get out, I'm not on a dating app, I don't want to meet my mom's candidate; I don't mix business and pleasure, and I'm patiently waiting in my house for my North Port Prince to ring the bell and save me. Life is unfair.

Regardless, I'm happy I experienced the craziness of the most significant theatre play of the year – Smarties parties, happy earthquakes. I get it now, except for two specific interactions that echoed in the crowded arena that I always think about.

The first one is what the crowd shouts when the mime is miming before the main character explains that she feels 52.

I will ask around if anyone remembers so I can add it below.

If I fail, make something up or, in Kalm's words, "Jog on!"

The second memory loss to recover is during the blood bath scene after the main character unveiled the shy "ghost":

Both moments live rent-free in my head. It was so cool; I wish I could have chimed in, too.

Unfortunately, my beginner-level Invictan language doesn't allow me to decipher the words, even after returning to my dozens of videos from that special theatre night.

For those wondering, it's indeed unfortunate that Ellie doesn't want to help me with this. She firmly believes that the hunt is fun. Is hunting by yourself fun, though? Having Smarties' fading voices in my head forever is not my idea of fun. Nevertheless, I have no regrets; I'm bringing all those awe-inspiring souvenirs to Camelia Street.

And here ends my Big Smoke City trip and my love letter to Smarties, who unwillingly uplifted me on a horrible day.

I'd also like to express my eternal gratitude to Mrs. Invictana for the fantastic and psychotic play. Thank you all.

Now, Smarties, please stop bothering the Invictan glory legend; she has better things to do than pleasing you, like baking cinnamon rolls and knitting a new scarf as she keeps forgetting hers in everyone's cabinets. She may even knit one for her friend The Llama to make sure he doesn't suffer from hypothermia.

***

Speaking of The Llama, he's doing an epic stunt at Jingle Wood forum, an Angel City venue. Nobody can stop him from cooking around. Doing five-course menus as if it were nothing is mental. Maybe he's not like us Xians.

He also brought Angel City's rivals together for the crazy after-show feast; everybody ate peacefully. Even Ross Eastbreak, usually picky with food, ate all the nuggets and left no crumbs. Outstanding achievements like that spark the crowd's euphoria and deserve respect.

During this time, The Dromedary was... *dromedaring*.

***

Enough about Starstrucks, let's turn the lights back on the current Invictus Land's leader, The Turtle. He just put a bet on a border restriction to prevent people from Nueva Luna Land from entering his territory. They call it the writing on the hidden wall.

That looks like something The Phoenix would do. Strange. Is everything okay with The Turtle? I hope it is.

What's not okay is people from the South of Invictus Land fearing devastating damage because of our planet's climatic tantrums.

The latter may result from soft parenting; now, Planet X is acting up, and no one can stop it. Again, watching *The Fate We Can't Escape*.

***

On a lighter note, the Triangulum Islands' Queen is... still not releasing new street art. After playing in our faces, she decided to play with our heads. I love her new short silver curls and her new bucket hat collection. Now can she please go back to the art studio and paint a damn painting? Don't tell me I'm a psychopath for still hoping.

Sorry, I had too many sleepless nights trying to finish this mess with a few days remaining; it's affecting my brain. She does her, and we do us, *gotcha*. I may as well create my damn painting studio as soon as I finish this hustle. Cheers to making my jokes come true!

What I admire most about Robean is her happy family with AceApp. I can't help thinking that maybe I should also give my non-existent best friend a chance. I'll never be ready for the five shades, but I can at least be a team player and learn about Huck Twang Girl's moves. Attagirl is now giving us advice in her podcast, and I'm rolling my eyes like G.I Jane.

Don't worry, I'm not a hater – no need to slap me unwillingly.

***

I love this world where the simplest things can change your life.

This wrap, written half-asleep, may as well reach a *Tales'* best-selling status if it gets leaked, and I wouldn't be surprised. That's not the goal. I would choose a little indie success over a worldwide frenzy any day. Why? My extreme kindness, my social anxiety, my paranoid personality disorder, and my intolerance of bullshit will ruin the show before it even starts.

On top of that, I know that my clumsiness will have me canceled faster than Huge Sane Bold runs. And if I'm as unlucky or irresponsible as pro swimmer Tim Lake, I might drink chlorinated water, drive, and get caught.

Dangerous behavior and a learned lesson for Tim Lake; nothing more to add. He's canceled now. What's the next step after cancellation? Being criticized and overanalyzed for everything, like the size of his eyes, if he tries to look aware and wide awake after a swim competition.

Too many lights on are not necessarily appreciated. Neither are extreme exhaustion and having insomnia like Cal Puccino.

I should have followed my lead on this; there is nothing more to add. Let's wish him (and me) healing, good luck, success, and happiness. It's all love in my fantasy world.

I should never get myself in his position because karma loves to teach judgmental people that what goes around always comes around. I'm no exception.

***

It's time to let go of my constant fear of what the future holds.

It won't be perfect, but I'm ready to let negative feelings fade and give way to my craziest dreams. Maybe one day I'll become a winner like Karl Alcatraz or Iggy Swisstech and receive a trophy as big as their Rolling Gardos' (Frawn Land's racket open).

While commenting on the results of the racket open, Sam told me I reminded her of Monta Crista. The legend says that the unknown woman was the victim of a conspiracy from people she trusted (*Huge mistake, Enormous!*), was wrongly imprisoned for crimes she didn't commit, then escaped and came back for revenge with a new face, new name, and an indecent amount of money. I get how I can relate to the unknown woman part of the story, but I can't imagine that comeback.

Even my dreams in a fantasy world seem limited. My 'what-ifs' always precede a 'never' or a 'not me.' Maybe there are kinds of craziness I haven't reached yet. I am determined to get there by the end of the year. Let's start now.

"What if I go to Cherry Land to become a neo-Samurai with my mentor, Keanolulu Breeze?"

"It's never going to happen."

"What if my damaged self could leave her crumbling domicile in GB Land to experience a crazier one in Invictus Land? I could become a worthy member of a bike rider gang chased by the Bad Lords' police. My biker's name could be Lady Moody."

"I could see anyone do that, not me."

It's not working yet; I would have too much afterthought about everything. Let's find out if I can broaden my imagination and believe more in the improbable possibilities.

In the meantime, here I am... still partying.

7

JULY

H ERE WE ARE... ESCAPING.

In July, catch me if you can!

Bye Juno! From now on, I will live my life to the fullest like Ellie –
minus the money.

I won't let bad news stop my fun and ruin the comic-con!

It's all or nothing, no regrets and no approval needed from my bank
account manager, Tamra J. Handsome! *Stop calling me.*

Tamra's worrying calls urging me to stop wasting money on trips
and start investing in financial products and real estate are stressing
me out. Not only that, but she keeps repeating that she also has alleged inside information that a puzzling Project XX25 is about to be
executed. Before I blocked her, she advised me to abandon checkers
and start playing 4D chess.

I don't understand what's going on. I have never played any of those games, and she sounds a little bit... crazy. She's not the only cuckoo person, as everyone is also talking about it. I'm blocking them all!

I only have three things on my mind: Sea, Text, and Sun!

You know the chorus: let's find ourselves in several lovely sceneries. I said, "No limit!"

***

Here I come, Scran Land (also known as Bull Land), the cradle of Scranish (or affectionately Bulliards), led conjointly by The Salmon and His Majesty The Bull. Scran Land's ruling system is similar to GB Land's, but culturally, it's strikingly reminiscent of Nueva Luna Land.

"¿Cómo estás?"

"Muy bien."

The weather and life here are ideal; I'm doing perfectly fine!

I thought I had found my new favorite spot until I learned tourists were attacked and no longer welcome here. My timing is always off. Let me channel my Violeta Dayvice and act the best I can, like the locals. No one better blow my cover with that lisp.

I plan to follow Scranish customs. First thing first, wake up late, let's say... noon. Then, I'll have my daily spicy *paylast* dish while listening to *fanenco* music. Also, I'll participate in cow rodeos every afternoon. Finally, it's nap time for me and 48 xillion people... until tapas time!

No, it's not. Surprisingly, some of my clichés were wrong. Scranish people are all hard workers who have faced multiple economic crises with a smile on their faces. Kudos to them. I could never. I need to rest. I'm only here for *el botellón*, and it's taking a toll on my body.

"*Despertarse Señora*"

"*¿Que dices? Patatas gravas, Berenjuevas* and *Perdón peppers* are ready?*

You better have *Bloodria* and Bloody Mary cocktails ready, too. But take your time to prepare it with pride and love; I have news to read."

***

Back to Invictus Land: Immunity is granted to The Phoenix by The Highest Court for all pending charges against him.

He was right to believe in a comeback. The red carpet is rolled out for him to achieve his dream to rule the world. He's hot to go on a sold-out Invictus Land's tour, with *huge* crowds.

A dramatic turn occurred while he delivered a speech in Keystone Land — one of Invictus Land's 13 'founder' territories.

Bombshell – an attempted senicide!

Allegedly, a disturbed distant Rojos relative decided to practice skeet shooting with The Phoenix as a target instead of the usual clay disc.

No one should laugh about this criminal and vile act. Instead, everyone should condemn it. It's not okay. I strongly believe that violence is never the solution. Why? The seemingly troubled and desperate young man paid the highest price for the atrocious offense: his precious journey on Planet X.

On the other hand, The Phoenix miraculously survives and raises his clenched wing as a symbol of Invictan victory, once again rising from its ashes. He's now a living legend!

This disturbing event has the entire world (his opponents included) questioning the professionalism of The Phoenix's Men-in-Wack security. Indeed, luckily, only the tip of The Phoenix's wing was injured, but it could have been otherwise as his cover wasn't properly assured, especially after the first hit.

Even before getting there, one can question why the crime perpetrator was left peacefully accessing a nearby rooftop party, drinking his bubble tea, shouldering his long-range bubble rifle, adjusting his shot, and shooting bubbles.

I find it boggling, even as a couch potato who has never worked a security-related job. But, hey! I'm not in the security field; maybe it's the norm. I'm just glad to hear that an investigation is underway to determine whether this is related to The Dandy's oily floor gate.

May the truth come forth.

This climax event, admittedly traumatic, may have just changed the course of The Phoenix's life and Invictus Land's ruling history by ricochet.

Only a few days after his attack, The Phoenix reveals his ride-or-die pick among Los Rojos' family – The Owl, the man whose values can do a 180° without hurting his head.

Regardless, stronger and wiser, The Phoenix officially accepts his title of Los Rojos' family leader in a moving 3-hour-long speech.

I almost shed a tear.

***

Fortunately, I had saved that tear for The Turtle's speech.

The current Invictus Land's leader just announced he's dropping out from the next ruling run. It's with great emotion that everyone thanks him for his tremendous efforts and sacrifices. They all wish him good luck, excellent balance, and rest.

He'll finally enjoy a long-awaited retirement in a few months, and he endorses his family's new leader, The Dolphin (or The Hyena for her detractors).

The Dolfin arrives in The Turtle's good graces and now must convince enough people in Invictus Land that she's the best solution to all their problems. It's not an effortless task, but she's up for this challenge.

***

Speaking of ruling tales, The Ram's term ends in my more peaceful Great Banter Land. The not-so-unanimous Prime Optimister didn't gather enough people for his cause, so he must leave the premises now. Indeed, the Grits changed their minds and now want another Optimister to rule. My lips are sealed about my vote.

Everybody, meet the replacement, The Kingfisher.

People keep pointing at differences between the two, but they are more similar than different to me. Neither can bend it like Dave; both look polite and are men – "potato, tomato." Anyway, congratulations, and good luck to the new deliverer!

There are more people to congratulate, as GB Land's racket open finals just finished. Windledown is always a great time. We had the pleasure of watching amazing games and spotting great attendees.

Among them, we were pleased to see a smiling Kountess with her kids, happy Tim Crazy, Zeneia with her outfit that never disappoints, Dave with his lucky cuff, and a pretty Dude, among others.

Well-deserved compliments go to Karl Alcatraz, who beat Nolack Jokeofwitch. It seems like no one can stop the rising racket star.

A little confession: I had never heard of him before this year, and my recluse self is still stuck in the rivalry between Radale Naval and Rogier Ferrare. I'm even restraining myself from mentioning older legends like Andrew Aghast, Born Cyborg, Peter Sampler, Elle Wells, Martha Nevrolova, or Stephanie Autograph – among others.

***

It's the ruling month, and we have breaking news from Red Dragon Land. Its leader, The Giant Red Panda, just revealed his plan to boost every sector for the next 5 years. I missed the part when this prominent Land started to struggle.

To me, it's one of the most powerful in the world. It might be a fable, but I heard we wouldn't be able to have most manufactured products without the greatness and dedication of its people, Dragonese. I'm referring to dystopian clothes, invisible phones, innovative energy, or flying vehicles, among other things.

I remember the story of a young man who was a special forces soldier, had an M.D. diploma, and finally became an astronaut, all while in his twenties. I couldn't help but make a shortcut and think that man could only be Dragonese. That's how highly I consider Dragonese genius minds. Anyway, I was wrong. The legend says that the man is actually from Invictus Land.

I now realize that if I need to shift my looser mentality, I only have two choices: a move to Red Dragon Land or Invictus Land.

***

While I hesitate, let's find another fabulous scenery on the hottest day in Planet X's history.

Here I come, Myths Land, part of Hope Union, the cradle of Mythelleners, led by The Shrew.

I can hear as-happy-as-a-sandboy people's rhythmic talks in one of its island's streets, protected by Lapis Lazuli-colored eyes:

"Γεια σας; (Yassas!)"

"γεια, πώς είσαι; (Geia, pós eísai!)"

"πολύ καλό ευχαριστώ (Polý kaló efcharistó), Τι κάνετε; (Ti kánete!)"

"Δεν μπορώ να παραπονεθώ. (Den boró na paraponethó)"

Did I arrive in paradise? I hope not; I am still too young for that, please.

Myths Land is just another chill environment with joyful people who are pleased to welcome everybody to the party. I want to slow down my traveling frenzy, but the sun is not letting me.

Let's enjoy the ride, then!

There's a different backdrop for every taste: white sand beaches, mountains, lakes, charming architecture, forests, and olive trees as far as the eye can see.

Luckily, I sold a kidney right before arriving so that I could afford to pay the bill at every place-to-be that Mythelenners advised me to try. Some spots are overpriced; others would make me voluntarily sell the remaining kidney to experience another night.

It reminds me of a past trip to Sin City, the artificial paradise of Invictus Land. I have experienced the best days of my life there.

I was staying at the Fantasy Hotel, which I heard is closing for good this month.

Nothing else has boosted my serotonin levels the way gambling for days there did. My road rage madness last year didn't even come close, and it was a bad one!

Crazier things happened in Sin City; I fell in love and temporarily married a stranger. Some people find it dumb because all I got from this is trouble, but others like me find it poetic – no wonder I am afraid of commitment now. All of it felt like a mirage or a Houdini-style illusion.

***

Speaking of Houdini, guess who's not back?

The great theatre illusionist, The Goat, is rumored to have disappeared since F5-category twisters hit the Land of Mad he was visiting. That's one bad news that detectives are investigating. A special squad is working on the case led by Deluwood's best detective, Ed Smurfy, and his Wowlywood partners, Santach and Charmash.

First, detectives inform the public that The Goat is a master of disguise and goes by different names: Slim Goaty, Mr. Mi-Name, or M&Aim – depending on his mood. None of his split personalities are pleasant, so he always sparks controversy.

Nevertheless, no one can say that the unapologetic adept in illusions is not one of the greatest in his craft, if not the greatest.

If he comes back from his intergalactic twister ride and reads this by coincidence on another planet, please, *pretty*, please, don't come for me.

Just in case, I'm pulling a Goaty-reverse card: I'm an overrated, annoying, and boring amateur who's culture-appropriating. I can add that I'm a four on a good day, and I should hit the gym instead of eating beans and drinking gin. I should also fix that face as quickly as possible.

If the attack comes my way anyway, I'll ask a hero to save me.

If Liepool or Werewolfine are free, they better not hesitate to rescue me on their way to the mani-petty spa.

If not, I'll take the canceled and drunk Huncook.

***

Speaking of rescue, I bet Ranan AllBeaming would not hesitate to come to Adakhi's rescue. Everybody knows they love each other to the money and back.

It's time for the grand wedding, and everybody is crying their heart out. This time, even a GB Land's former Optimister – The Sloth, El Jefe, Joe Scena, Priceyankee, and husband Neack Jokas joined the festivities.

After Queen V and Robean, we may have had a Nadelle performance if she wasn't on a farewell tour in Geranium Land's Forthright City. Too bad. Maybe the next heir of the AllBeaming family will have that chance.

One up-and-coming actress was free to give a toast, but right before the ceremony, she missed her flight to Golden Sparrow Land because she drank her beer instead of asking someone to hold it – a little mistake from the young Ingreat Distress. Maybe she can heal and learn resilience from the great, the only Selene Diamond.

***

Joyous news from Frawn Land: the Olyxiad games, where all Lands compete in fun games, just opened with famous singers Lady Mama and Selene Diamond.

An infamous nightmarish opening followed: from decapitated heads and spartan lady to spicy scenes including Flurfs served on a platter, Frawnchies showed no limit to their creativity. *Bravo, oui!*

We love Flurfs, but we wouldn't eat them – not even if they turned into candies. Come on! We heard they would eat us, though, so everyone should stay away from the only uncontacted indigenous people on Planet X! Indeed, the few things we know about Flurfs is that they are little blue gnomes living in magical flowers and vegetables in hidden enchanted forests of North Forbidden Land (–; –).

Let's not make it about them; it's the Olyxiads, and everybody's happy to see ambassadors' bestie duo from Invictus Land – Swoop Dodge and Bertha Steward.

Congratulations to the most talked-about winners: Gabe Tomats, Neo, Liles, Leo Merchant, Torre Husky, Reagen Smitt, the Invictan acrobats' Golden Girls, Invictus Land's Binball's "Fantasy Team" led by The Brown, and no-gear sharpshooter Yousoof Disketch (also known as *Blond, Yousoof Blond*).

Gold, Silver, Bronze, and participation trophy winners should all be proud of their incredible achievements.

Especially when you understand that years of training are judged by a few seconds or minutes on D-day, the amount of self-control and composure they need not to panic and excel in this specific moment differentiates the goods from the greats and the amateurs from the professionals.

The idea of someone being able to do something perfectly a thousand times during a year but being judged on a mistake for the 1001st time is challenging to grasp for me.

I'm good at functioning under pressure and keeping my cool, but most of the time, I will quit before putting myself in a life-or-death situation.

I'm surprised I even made it to the end of July. I don't know if I will reach the end of the year, but I'm willing to try.

In the meantime, here I am... still escaping.

8

AUGUST

HERE WE ARE... TOASTING.

There's no escaping August's heat and its furtive memories.

It's a tricky month: one foot in the present excitement, one foot in the unavoidable future sadness.

For people who fear goodbyes and farewells, it's time to be a stalwart.

I wish I could feel Smarties' euphoria during this phase of mine, but I feel exactly like the gelato I'm holding – melting.

Still, in Frawn Land's Olyxiads, the host presents a new game: glass breaking.

Sunburnt Land introduces its most fantastic glass breaker, meet Gratchel Gun (known as Raygaroo). The stupor is considerable in the face of her unconventional glass-breaking techniques.

Some argue that she outshined other gamers more deserving of the fame by doing so. This conundrum can apply to every subject in life. Should people dim their light so that others can reach the same level? I don't think so; it would be unfair. If I wanted to write a book, I wouldn't ask all actual authors to stop writing so that my art has any chance of being read. If it deserves oblivion, then oblivion it is.

I don't think we should mither over Raygoroo's performance here. She did compete, both at home and in Olyxiads. If anyone should be criticized, it's Sunburnt Land's so-called best glass breakers who didn't attend the local contest and the glass-breaking committee for not making righteous calls when necessary.

People should never count on a fearless artist to back down. Also, the media and everybody who watched the massacre could have made it a no-brainer. Instead, everybody preferred to talk about it and amplify her impact.

So, here she is, running like HeKnowsSpeed and hopping like a kangaroo in my script. Kudos to her!

To make it come full circle, watching that Huck Twang Girl interview Raygaroo on her podcast would be the icing on the cake.

And that closes the great Olyxiad games.

Luckily, Selene Diamond responded again to Frawnchs' rescue call for the closing ceremony.

After the criticism of the opening, they went for more classic and futuristic artistry, including the handover to the next host, Invictus Land.

The great, the impossible, Tim Crazy made a daring stunt, forewarning the great show to come to Invictus Land in four years.

In the closing ceremony, Frawnchies also included a scene of a mysterious flying horse's rider covered with a black cape. At first, I thought it was Queen V. Then, I wondered if it could be Mrs. Invictana... But we never had a revelation. Maybe it was one of them, or both.

However, what was revealed this year is Selene's fight for a healthy life, causing her excruciating pain. After a long period of suffering, better days seem ahead of her. Her iconic and indelible performance at the top of the Lady of Steal was a good way back in the spotlight. It's a kind of spotlight that would be deplorable for me, considering the extreme scrutiny she faces.

Luckily, that will never be the case. I will continue my modest life and overcompensate my fears with travels and parties until I decide to face them.

Let's do what we do best: find ourselves *in* good scenery.

Here I come, Italic Land (also known as Beautiful Boot Land), the cradle of Italicans (or affectionately Fingertipers) and led by The Canis.

"Buongiorno principessa, come sta?"
"Tutto bene, grazie. E tu?"
"La vita è bella."

For some reason, if I see a winery around, it feels like home.

No, I'm kidding. I'm here to experience what Italicans call the *Dolce Vita*. I guess I can continue to wake up late. Let's switch the main dish to daily pasta for lunch and pizza for dinner.

If only I knew it was the blue zone's secret to a longer life expectancy, I would have eaten instant noodles and frozen pizzas earlier.

Let's hope no Fingertiper will read this, as I know it will feel like a dagger in their hearts – the same way cutting spaghetti or adding fresh cream in Chef Pupone Tutti's Carbonara hurts. I didn't even dare to use the modern name of this ancient dish, as I know my adored and proud Italicans are extremely sensitive.

Still, anyone who finds this too hurtful should try to blink twice to ensure they're alive. In case of doubt, a little glass of *Chiante* or *Monti* will make the pain go away... or not.

Speaking of pain, the world is saddened and shocked by tragic news coming from Beautiful Boot Land's southern coast guards.

Close to where I am, a waterspout that occurred during a flash storm led to the capsize of a luxury Sea Lion. Half a dozen people were tragically forced to explore Argo Navis. There is no need to get into the conspiracy theories that surfaced; may all their crafts rest in peace, and may their families find the strength to overcome the devastating departure.

Note to self: take no thought of the morrow.

***

I presume it's the right time to check the news feed while I bask in my *aperitivo* and wine-tasting.

It appears I'm not the only one playing hide-and-seek.

From Region IV (+; –), Rivers Land's Optimister just fled her territory after scandals arose. She reminds me of someone dear to my heart. Catch her if you can.

***

One who's not playing and not hiding is The Dolphin.

She's finding her feet and breaking new ground in *SYTYCR*.

As expected, Los Blaus family's second musical chairs game occurs between Pretzel, Shakiro, Copper, Busheer, Ketty, and – spoiler alert – the winner... The Labrador.

Say his name out loud, no half measure, as The Labrador is screaming, "I won!"

Few people know that enjoying the dance with a smile, playing nice, having no strategy, and avoiding evil schemes are the keys to winning musical chairs. Those too focused on eliminating other contestants tend to miss the crucial moment when the music stops, stay between chairs with their tails betwixt their legs, and lose.

All things considered, The Dolphin's new trusty partner is the perfect choice to work with side-by-side for the upcoming double potato sack race.

It's time for the cerebral and mirthful Dolphin to formally accept her nomination as Los Blaus' leader for *SYTYCR*. Her acceptance speech is phenomenal, and the celebratory night doesn't disappoint.

My agoraphobic self would not have survived; it is impossible to know and name them all; there are just way too many people.

The "who's who" of "love that" is here: Patricia LaBale, Comma, DJ Coffeedy, Wendale Pearce, Big John, and Strike Lean, among others.

Everything we see about the union between the two is reminiscent of Smarties parties: joyful, loving, and respectful.

The next game – the roll call, comprises the duo riding tandem across Invictus Land to call all lovers and voters.

The honorific bike ride culminates in a spectacular week-long party with the help of Rhanan and Adakhi's event planner, Kay 'Chi-Chi-Chic' Ly.

If The Dolphin's official endorsements started with a shy brat, now she's all the rage, and Very Important People from the Blau clan will be in attendance.

Obviously, The Labrador is present with his beautiful family, and they should be protected at all costs.

The Oracle is not here, but the buffet is open, and everybody wants to give a toast.

It's their pleasure to welcome former Invictan leader The Heron back to the spotlight for the greater good. He took the opportunity to remind Invictans that "teamwork makes the dream work, and even though our divergence matters, our unity matters more."

I was teary-eyed but hollered when he added: "No, I did not have a platonic relationship with that Galer woman; we were not even FRIENDS."

I'm glad he hasn't lost his sense of humor, but I'm even more delighted to see another former leader toasting – class act, The Bear. He accolades the current leader for always supporting and respecting democracy despite the challenges. The Bear then points out what's at stake: "Invictans need a leader who can fight for them." He doubts The Phoenix has what it takes, but he's confident that The Dolphin does. The party guests agree and start chanting, "Yes, she can."

Moved by his words, The Turtle joins him for the toast and adds that he fears *bad* blood with The Phoenix, who he believes has dicta-torship desires. While sipping his sparkling wine, he continues with a memorable speech. The jokes are flowing, from calling himself "older than a dinosaur" to calling The Phoenix a loser and a *sucker*; he would give John Carlyle and Gerard Prior a run for their money. Maybe he thought it was 'Your Mama' contest instead of *SYTYCR*; go figure. Whether one agrees with his ruling method and choices, it's difficult not to express admiration for his dedication and commitment until the end, despite struggling. People are easy to judge, but few would sacrifice their precious time on Planet X for the common good.

I know I can't, and I'm resolved not to abandon my dreams for anyone's good. But at least I stopped complaining and sitting around, as The Dolphin's mom would advise. I am doing something; I'm writing these words right now; I'm becoming more active than passive.

But enough about me, back to my favorite moment.

The Bear indirectly roasted The Phoenix's obsession with name-calling, conspiracy theories, and crowd... ..sizes.

There is a round of applause for The Bear and a standing ovation for his wife, The Deer, who follows for the next toast. Demure and charming as usual, she lets *shawties* go low and lower while *she* chooses her signature high road. She's such a brilliant orator who beautifully condemns hideous, misogynistic, and xenophobic lies allegedly spread by the opposite family. She can hardly imagine Los Rojos working to make Invictans' lives better, as they allegedly plan to control women's bodies, shut down educational institutions, cut people's healthcare, and demonize tenderness enthusiasts for who they love. Fired up, The Deer then exits and gives a little kiss to her favorite thoughtful guy, her honey – The Bear. If you had forgotten they invented love, that's your booster shot.

Can Invictus and Planet X go back to that? No, they can't.

Invictans need to trust the process and respect democracy.

The "who's who" of "say that" would agree, and they are here: Rev. Sharp, Minnie Calling, Keyman, Dame O'Purple, Eve Lingering, Alex

Courteous, Steven Coldbeer, and Carrie Warrington with her fantasy spouse Anthony Goodwill, among others.

Let's not forget the praised poet who shared some wisdom. No, it wasn't Mrs. Invictana who was busy baking cookies and dealing with her *Auras*. Instead, Almond Worman – an acclaimed and certified poet, shared some needed wisdom.

The "who's who" of "shout that" are adding their insight, too: John Regent, Stevia Wonda, The Chics or Marie Lories, among others.

Then, the public was teased about a mother-daughter duo speech to come. Spectators watching the show held their breath, waiting for Queen V and Yellow to appear. All hopes felt flat as the public realized they weren't there but leapt when Ro!se and her lovely daughter Bravow delivered an inspiring and loud speech. Everybody raised their glasses to the good old days.

Finally, The Dolphin concluded with a touching speech, expressing how she will work to bring peace to Holy Land and how she anguishes the idea of giving more power to an alleged convicted opponent.

She further states that if Invictans choose not to go back to The Phoenix era, they might be at the dawn of the patriarchy's end, a new way forward to freedom, empathy, dignity, justice, and endless opportunities. Some are sold on this Invictus dream, and the fun party ends with glitter in the air.

***

The following episodes of *SYTYCR* are dedicated to Los Rojos' roll call. The Phoenix is determined to win Invictans' hearts even more so after cheating a one-way galaxy exploration only a few days earlier. Armed with a noticeable white bandage on his left wing, the triumphant leader of Los Rojos recounts the incident with impactful words: "I shouldn't be standing here today." The... .crowd cheers and welcomes him with their favorite slogans: "We love The Phoenix! Make Invictus Strait Again!"

With that begins his celebratory week-long party after his honorary bike ride.

Usually keeping a low profile, his mysterious and elegant wife – The Osprey – is surprisingly here to support him. Accompanied by their son – The Bison, she gives a short toast. The Osprey reminds the public that she's been by The Phoenix's side through ups and downs, primarily because he's a genuine, caring, and charitable man who inspires all Invictans. She also explains how traumatizing and devastating it was for them to learn about the incident that almost cut short her husband's passion for music, dance, and laughter.

I can admit that his signature dance is my kryptonite.

Following her for additional toasts is Porter Navejo, The Phoenix's former personal shopper, who is freshly released from detention.

He was allegedly serving a crime related to a Cyber Monday scam.

The now tattooed MISA supporter warns the public that Big Brother exposed his crimes and will likely expose theirs. Unimpressed by alleged intimidation from the Blaus, he proudly asserts that injustice brought by The Turtle will never break him or The Phoenix.

He then gives the mic to Jam Judge, who reads a poem about the power of love, and that makes everyone smile.

What makes everyone laugh is the aquarium he brought to showcase his adored baby shark. People who didn't know there were fun folks on Los Rojos' side now know. Even Picky Haler, who used to condemn The Phoenix's every move, now calls for unity and collaborative efforts to increase the size of her newly found family.

Speaking of family, the public can watch a short dance video starring Camille – The Phoenix's beautiful granddaughter – who explains her grandfather is not a bad person.

She recounts struggling in school one day, and The Phoenix picked her up to lift her mood. She calls it "the best day with him playing chess on a golf course." What an endearing family! I wish I could still do fun things with my grandfather, too. Don't pity me; that's just life.

Camille's dad, The Phoenix Jr., hugs her and takes over the toast. He makes it short; he's ready to Make Invictus Strait Again and is so proud of his dad, "the greatest leader that ever lived."

Then we have, just like at Los Blaus' party, the "who's who" of "say that" coming to toast one after the other.

The Owl and his supporting wife – The Peafowl – arrived late. Inspired by The Labrador's *Rumba Fast-Food* visit, they made an awkward "OK" stop to buy cronuts at a local shop to bring to the party. While his wife wants to show her gratitude for everybody's trust and support, The Labrador is here to reassert that The Phoenix's minimalist and innovative vision is Invictus Land's only recourse to save people's hopes and dreams. The goal is to give the lead role to Invictans and "Make Invictus Strait Again." The charming couple – who also invented love, cheers to the deserving working class and exits the toasting stage while holding hands.

Then, we can watch the harrowing joint toast given by Park Robertson and West Aunt, the natives from Chocolate City. They're here to get the party started and tell their stories, how they went from hardship to opulence, from disadvantaged to privileged.

It's inspiring to learn how someone can go from normal struggling people, bankrupt and evicted, to a thriving coaching life. They state facts with or without receipts: "In The Phoenix's era, the Invictan dream was real, hope was allowed, the economy was thriving with affordable housing, low-priced gas and high employment rate with manufacturing jobs protected."

If The Bear was there, I can bet my small bank account that he would have added, "That's MY economy I gave him," and his wife would have agreed with her signature nod.

Anyway, the list of toasters goes on and on, so I dissociate, and I only spot Daniel Black, Bruce Banter, Marge T. Grey, Mussel Rant, Tan Blite and Chamber Groove with her tattooed cheeks for the people.

The "who's who" of "shout that" for Los Rojos are also significant: Mid Rogue, Leroy Greyhoods, House DJ Michael Jobson, FifthFire and Boris Gianon.

Finally, The Phoenix concludes the party displaying his great oratory qualities while the crowd chants "Fighter."

He's determined to fight hate and pay homage to the collateral damage caused by the vile act that he survived.

He wants Invictans to use this traumatic event to remind them they share a common life purpose: faith, freedom, and fairness.

With these touching words and the fabulous party, I might also be sold on this dream!

The Phoenix may be on the right track to win Invictans' hearts as his family fully supports him, and even former opponents like KJR join forces to boost his chances.

***

Speaking of regaining strength, great news from Great Banter Land: Her Grace The Kountess is looking good and doing better as she manages to join her family at Choir Service. Always elegant, I can't help but make a parallel with The Deer's allure, so demure.

***

Life's short and should always be the priority.

I suddenly see flowers bloom everywhere.

I stop, look at three little birds chirping, and snap photos of poppies, my favorites. When I feel sad, seeing them will always brighten my day. It's not Ellie's favorites at all; she's rather fond of zinnias.

The saying "opposites attract" also works with friends.

It's funny how Ellie felt a stroke of serendipity when I told her that in January, a Tales City's guide informed me it's her idol Rumor Girl's favorites, too. She's stoked, so I feel obliged to tell her every tale the guide shared about the girl.

There's trouble in paradise, and Rumor Girl is having her fair share of drama with Giudizio, her tabloid co-founder and head of editorial content.

Before that, the most recent information I had was her being tone-deaf about Her Grace The Kountess' struggles, but she apologized for being clumsy.

Toot sweet, we might have an explanation of why Rumor Girl didn't attend the *Meet & Greed Gala*, as she seems to have lost her sense of fashion. We also realize that the woman might never have had a sense of humor as we get the chance to witness a *#throwback* to all her alleged missed jokes: commenting on an infertile woman's non-existent baby bump, offering diapers to a lactose-intolerant lady, casually sitting on a couch while joking about the advice she would give to an IPV victim, mocking a caged bird or getting married on a Lily of the Valley flowers' plantation. Sorry, the latter doesn't count because her husband Breyan allegedly blamed a defective algorithm and a not-so-thoughtful wedding planner.

Let's forgive and forget all that.

While Rumor Girl looks out of time and is ready to promote her merch (from clean-air products to Yummy-branded beverages), her partner Giudizio seems serious, empathetic, and sincere. I fear that with critics emerging, it's just the beginning of mission damage control on her side.

As a good wannabe Taler, I won't cross that line and fall into the trap of trying to find out who's the instigator in all this mess, because it always ends with fuss.

***

Another slippery line I don't want to dance on with my beautiful boots is Jane Loe and Bun Affect's relationship (a couple infamously known as Bunane). These acclaimed real estate agents form a specific pair of love inventors: those who invented love twice. Jackpot!

You might wonder how one can invent the same thing twice. Comparing it to anything you own that has several versions, variants, or upgrades might do the trick, that's them.

Like Enchanti and Naily, they're brighter than the late Steave Works. The difference between the two pairs is mainly in how they were received by those who cared.

Bunane's rekindle has been side-eyed since it was announced. Then they got themselves a sumptuous scenery and got married. People were glad for them and hoped they would stay together forever because they seemed to be each other's ride-or-die.

Bun started to look more miserable by the minute, while Jane seemed on cloud nine. Some were quick to call it red flags, but I know reality spin exists, so I was still hoping for the best.

I admit I knew *sheets* would hit the fan when I saw Bun storming Tim Broady's birthday, acting like a fool on live TV and ranting about his haters.

So, let's get to the point: after a few months of not-so-unfounded speculations, the couple announced they are splitting and want everybody to respect their privacy.

Without asking for it, we had front-row access to Jane's privacy on her real estate show, and now we are being requested not to infringe on it. "OK," people got the memo and even decided not to go to her open houses, fearing she might feel stalked there. Jane, whose story from "the block" is yet to be corroborated, then canceled all her upcoming real estate events, citing "a sudden desire and need to spend time with her family."

Again, who am I to judge? Even my craziest dreams don't come closer to any of the complex challenges Jane had to face to achieve one of the world's most remarkable real estate careers.

Yes, she may have relied on her team to find properties to sell, host open houses, and find a buyer, but her name is still on that sale contract, and that's what matters. Even the best would agree.

Maybe I should ask Morizzio Humanske, Frederic Oakland, Gosh Haltman, or Joch Flagged. Are they even the best, or are they just marketable influencers? We might never know.

At least some good news for Bun: there's always a Jane on the side, ready to save him from his demons. Hide your Janes! On-Off, In-Out, they're all alright.

***

I know I shouldn't be proud of calling that Bunane split. But considering my not-so-glorious year, that one thing I got right in all my predictions should be viewed as a win.

My defective crystal ball didn't see Justice Beaver and his wife's welcoming of baby Jazz, but we never know; Aliens invading my mind right now might be the second valid prediction. Let's hope not.

In retrospect, it always comes back to love and my unsuccessful attempt to settle down so far. Let's empathize with anyone who suffered from disillusioned love, even if I can't relate.

I might as well stick to my knitting.

It's cocktail o'clock, and all this love talk got me thirsty, so I ask the bartender to pour me my special Spirit cocktail drink: in a crystal glass, add the necessary amount of your favorite *Spumante*, the same amount of your favorite digestive bitter liquor, squeeze a lemon into it and decorate with a slice of peach. It goes without saying that it's delicious – as splendid as the *contadino* sitting at the bar and staring at me with his dark eyes. I know a great night ahead when I see one.

After all the bars closed, I realized it was the end of the day and we were getting closer to the end of the month.

It felt good to try and live for a few months without being obsessed with conforming to society's standards.

From that, I concluded I wouldn't change a thing about the decisions I made in the past and the way things are right now.

Yes, it might be time to shoulder the responsibility for my actions and hold myself accountable for choosing to party instead of working on ways to achieve all the dreams and promises made at the beginning of the year.

In the meantime, here I am... still toasting.

9

September

HERE WE ARE... THINKING.

Wherever you are, September brings you back.

A long way home...

Back to blue for adults like me and back to school for the candid youth.

It's okay, I'm okay; I survived a few farewells and goodbyes.

I now wish the same for every crying person I pass by at the airport for my return flight.

I thought I had seen it all. Am I interrupting a movie set, or is it reality?

"I can't let go, Love."

"You'll have to, or you'll miss your flight, Honey."

"I know you can't afford to travel soon, so I'll come back as soon as I have some time off from work. Wait for me, okay?"

"I'll wait, but don't stress about it. I believe in destiny. If it's meant to be, it will happen."

"I believe you're my destiny, and I can only picture my white picket fence house with you. I Love You."

"Thank you. Go! You're running out of time. Don't miss your flight." (*air kiss*)

I'm not a fortune teller or a seer, but I can predict that airport relationship's future better than meteorologists are forecasting weather changes. Again, please note that I don't thrive on schadenfreude. I just have found something I'm good at; relationship projection.

I took a trip down memory lane to search for one time I acted that erratically; I couldn't find any.

I'm the can of worms, I'm emotionless, I lack passion.

Working on it, though, apparently there are magic herbs and tea that could fix me. If not, I'll find a podcast to cure my apathy.

I happen to understand for the first time that saying about age and wisdom.

Bad news: I'm getting old.

Good news: I was already very detached emotionally and now my emotions and I are not on the same planet anymore.

The force of attraction is pushing me closer to the Moon, to the second act, to my prophecy: I will end up a lonely cat lady.

I wish I could say otherwise, but the only thing left to do is find a cat or two – or so many I can't count.

How should I choose the breed? Maybe I should ask Mrs. Invictana, who is an expert on the matter. Unfortunately, I don't have her number.

There are so many to choose from: Invictan curl, Invictan wirehair, Grit shorthair, Chartered, Exotic shorthair, Cherrynese bobtail, etc. My main focus is "adopt, don't buy," and as seen on the Xieta Verse, if someone faints in a cat shop, it must be a diversion to steal a rare and "valuable" kitten.

Hush now.

We never know, if a lovely reader finds this knowledge transfer after getting lost in *The Jungle*; prithee, don't get influenced by my postmodern desperation. Instead, take the vow to closely follow the journey of *your* life. Hoping it's brighter than my Grit, grey days.

If you don't want to fall into the broken-ones' well, you should run. Just like I am about to do.

Welcome back, globetrotter spirit. Let's find ourselves a resplendent scenery.

I'm free; here I come, Gold Tiger Land, cradle of Tigerati, led by His Emir The Oryx.

If I had to find one photo to illustrate the saying "rags to riches," it would be a photo of this fascinating and lavish place.

I feel wealthy; my assigned driver, Waleed, opens the door of the limousine and greets me:

"Marhaba. Alhan wa sahlan."

"Marhaba. Kaeefhalak."

"Tamaam, shukran. AshoofookBukra. Maasalaamah."

"Tabaan. Maasalaamah."

Over 50 years ago, Gold Tiger Land was an underdeveloped but culturally rich desert. Then, they struck all kinds of oils. The rest is history, from catching drips and chasing dreams to building wonders.

If you want to experience glamour and high-end luxury without selling a few organs, it's the right place.

Hot tea under extreme heat, gold souk, belly dance performance, camel, and 6x6 dune rides are reminiscent of my trip to Mother Land. What's different is... money – shedloads of cash.

Maybe that's where Monta Crista's Treasured Safe has been hidden by her tutor in the legend. I can easily retrieve the safe if the treasure hunt does not require a walk on a glass floor 1500 meters above ground or climbing the world's highest skyscraper like Tim Crazy. I get dizzy just by the thought of it while I enjoy the magnificent fountain show.

I'm still good at multitasking; let's check the latest fantasy news.

***

Sad news from Mother Land: a Love City Olyxiads winner tragically departed Planet X because of her boyfriend's cowardly and senseless act. She's a loving mother, a young, vibrant, and talented champion whose legacy thankfully will continue to endure.

Her appaling story highlights once again the recurrent violence against women that is either rising or being more talked about. And when we think we've seen it all, we have another example of an unmasked, evil kind of man dressed as Dom Juan.

From Frawn Land, The Pelican's story perfectly exemplifies ordinary life's evil. This surreal trial is the story of a woman who mistakenly thought she shared the most incredible love with her husband of 50 years. But the deranged and dangerous man most unimaginably betrayed her and their daughter.

It may have been better for her to lose her mind than uncover the truth. Medical gaslighting at its best: no one listened to her for 20 years.

Luckily, the despicable man was slightly more stupid than evil as he succumbed to the thrill of another crime in broad daylight. A security guard allegedly spotted him upskirting women in an open-air market, reported him, and encouraged the victims to speak out and press charges. It's a crucial moment in this gruesome case.

The Pelican could have been rescued earlier, but better late than never, a feminist hero is born. Her choosing to reveal her face so that her alleged 100+ oppressors experience the fear and shame usually felt by victims is the reason she is The Pelican.

In the legend, the majestic bird symbolizes rebirth, wisdom, sacrifice, and maternal love. It is said that pelicans resurrect their offspring with their own blood, the same way The Pelican gives hope and courage to all the unknown victims and gives light to all unspoken crimes.

Not all men, but again, even in fantasy, it's impossible to enjoy a simple silly moment without being interrupted with devastating news.

Some people believe it's a woman's world; I wonder what it would be if it weren't.

Would we end up marrying Aliens like Dobrina Esprenter?

I long hesitated to include lousy news, but we agreed just to suck it up, right? That's life, and if The Pelican finds the strength to smile and carry on with her life, I can't do less.

***

Speaking of bright smiles, perfect teeth are the only common denominator among Invictans – including opponents of the ruling race.

The Dolfin is now showing she's one bold woman as she enters her first debate against The Phoenix.

The brave lady promises to represent a new leadership generation, exempt from lies and exclusion. She lets everyone know she dislikes The Phoenix and his small rallies.

I can admit that seeing a thumb down in real life felt refreshing, as I've been secretly working on solving its disappearance for a few years. Indeed, like ratio matters and I refuse to believe that everything is now either liked... or liked. Having only one option may increase positivity but lacks objectivity and realism.

The Phoenix counterattacks with a thumb up, claiming that The Dolfin and The Turtle are the main reasons consumer prices are sky-rocketing. He dodges the debate about size, as he has "the biggest rallies," and there's no doubt about that.

He continues with new scandalous theories about people eating ants, bats, cats and dogs. The Dolphin's race pace is brought up, too. She's a dolphin, not a shark; the debate is closed.

***

Another debate I'd like to close once and for all is whether The Phoenix won five years ago. But we can't always get what we want.

That's what I tell to every kid I encounter.

It takes a village to raise children; I'll do anything for my young nieces and nephews.

As far as I'm concerned, I only need *SYTYCR* winner to allow me to visit Invictus Land without fearing ending up in some crossfire when shopping or dropping off Ellie's kids at school.

That's something The Phoenix just avoided again; the lucky man deserves a gold statue.

Allegedly, the new wannabe hitman charged for the foiled attack against The Phoenix used to be a good Samaritan who was working on housing homeless people. He was a former supporter of The Phoenix in the past, but he radically changed his view and started a vigilante mission aimed at hurting him.

I'll continue to mind my business while most forecasts predict The Dolfin as the subsequent LOTIS (Leader Of The Invictan Soil).

***

Speaking of winning, Giani Wrongdoer wins the men's *Grand Slap* tournament in Invictus Land – the first time in history for an Italican. You'd better spend your life on your best behavior with that kind of name. At least, no one should be surprised by any wrongdoing by him. Never mind, on the women's side, Arya Salsalenka takes the trophy home.

Both winners gave their all to each slap, while cameras spotted a few famous faces in the building: Malone couple, the Aim cis & Co, Mrs. Invictana wearing a mansion-on-the-prairie dress, and Wild Valentine having a blast joined at her hip.

My claustrophobic self's urge to break the chain anytime it gets too clingy might never get the chance to experience this wild side of love under a blue sky.

The individually successful couple is on a well-deserved break and might hint at a singing career debut. I don't like it. I don't like change. I just got on board with her theatre performances; I wouldn't want to switch gears and end up in no-man's-land.

A little confession: I can enjoy the darkness of a romantic drama act, but I hate love songs. Maybe because I'm way too good at breaking my own heart, I don't need them. Big hug to anyone as messed up as me who also thinks that real life is hard enough.

Mrs. Invictana's life doesn't seem too complicated, at least.

She had some help to organize a space trip to explore our four little moons orbiting our planet, and she thanked her BOYFRIEND while landing with her co-pilot – Postman.

She can do it all, and her Wild Valentine can turn anything into platinum.

I can't wait for him to start a podcast to teach us all how to make it rain, legally and with class, please.

***

Maybe that's the beginning of my new fairytale life, which I deserve.

In front of me now are open seas of opportunities and dreams. I can hear the sound of my internal gong: here's to smiling, never being tired, building my mountain to climb, and no more losing!

I can already see myself in the *landside*, on a tractor, in endless greenery, and calling my former colleagues to tell them: "I miss you. I envy you. I don't mean it." Pure pleasure.

I might even have it embossed on my pair of boots.

In all honesty, if my family and friends could see me now, they would section me. With a little chance, by the time they read this, I will be better than ever and ready for myself.

Please give me a reason to plunge into fantasy, and I'll be out, gone with the wind with my fellow Uglies!

One who's far from being ugly is the stunning fashionista Taverne Fox. Love her! I need a confidence class from her and all contacts from her glam squad. The sooner, the better!

****

Regarding wind, hurricane Elena reached Category 4 when it hit Invictus' southern Sunshine City. Doing so took a massive toll on Invictan lives – with hundreds of casualties, thousands of injured, and xillions affected by electricity shortage and property damage.

It's the second most impactful hurricane after Ekaterina, and we all still remember its name. We all remember how, almost 20 years ago, the destructing hurricane ripped Big Easy City apart.

Another consequential phenomenon is expected to strike Big Easy City in Dreizember this year: NSL's Super Masked Ball will be held there, and The Llama has been chosen as the headliner for the live cooking show.

Critics arose more than applause while an unfinished beef slice was getting cold on Starstrucks' countertop.

Some people were routing for Chef Lil Whale – the native from Big Easy City, but it would have been too easy for the event planner. That's the paradox of choice.

Nonetheless, the foodie Pink Doll alleged that The Jeydi who is coordinating the event's live filming, is primarily responsible for Lil Whale's snub.

How brave of Pink Doll to show her rebel side and burn an already fragile bridge between her and success. Let's hope that she won't be blackballed or go M.I.A.

*****

Speaking of the devil, these are methods allegedly used by The Dandy instead. Yes, he's back, but not doing the shoulder-shake dance this time. The Bad Lords' police arrested him in Tales City and charged him with serious accusations.

Like The Pelican's husband, if proven guilty, he'll deserve the highest sentence.

He dared to deny his ex-girlfriend Classy Cherry's accusations, and reality checks proved him wrong.

At least, he faced his judgment for this one and didn't flee to Godly Island, as Rushell Summons did.

Maybe one of Holy Land's leaders should have also fled to Godly Island to escape the fatal attack against him – prayers and thoughts for him to enjoy an eternal and peaceful celestial cruise.

Like I said, I don't take sides.

I still hope for better days and enjoyable pink skies in Holy Land.

*****

On a happier note, I'm delighted to announce that Her Grace The Kountess has just finished her precautionary treatment. Pages are turning, hard times may fade away, and she can consider a slow return to work. The demure fighter, her husband, His Grace The Kount, and their sweet and short minis are enjoying life.

***

Without warning, my intrusive thoughts kick in, and I start thinking about Lucy's Tree, hoping no one cut it to build a wolf sanctuary or an innovative megalopolis project.

Whatever, just like one of my friends in great distress, I quit my addictions and am continuing my new sober life. It has me ordering organic beet juice with a splash of ginger, which is slowly transforming me into the pigtails Vikeen girl. Next thing you know, I may start a green strike, throw orange paint on random supersonic planes or art like Da Vinctus' *Joy Conde*. It's not the kind of change I'm counting the days for.

***

What I've longed for is the return of Linked Parking group after an understanding break. The adored CEO Chastor is replaced by Ely Handstrong. Maybe not a woke choice or a DVI (Driving Very Intelligently) hire, I think – just doomed if they chose the perfect clone, doomed if they didn't. As long as I have enough space to parallel park, I'm fine. At least it's different and I'm okay with it; even if I just said I don't like change.

I guess I'm no different than my siblings arguing in the room next door; perfectly imperfect.

Speaking of clones, Invictans and the world watching are witnessing new groundbreaking scientific developments – the first successful full golden-eye and diamond face transplant.

I might be closer to my Monta-Crista moment than ever before.

In the meantime, here we are… still thinking.

10

OCTOBER

HERE WE ARE... SINKING.

October's existential dread is every overthinker's nightmare.

It's that time of the year when the universe wishes us ladies to "break a leg." The entire town is painted pink in honor of all warrior princesses fighting the Big K.

I don't want to compare my mild suffering to theirs, but I landed back from Gold Tiger Land with a sore throat and a runny nose.

Meet Lady Seely Clown in her sick era.

What a way to start the October Slide. Considering the amount of preventative tea with honey I drank, I shouldn't be in this position.

Let's monitor old patterns: watering eyes, coughing fits, and achy muscles. Dirty luck, this is not my first rodeo, and I'm getting more knowledgeable than my general practitioner, so my medicine cabinet at home is well stocked.

Remember, I'm an untrained amateur; please don't try this at home and consult an actual M.D. instead of asking everybody's favorite know-it-all browser – the one and only Goodle!

You can call me too if you're highly delusional and scareless.

I try to crack jokes while fever and extreme fatigue can't even let me think of the next scenery that will cure me. So, I'm stuck in bed with my emotional baggage. I'm now reconsidering all my life choices. I would be an ER doctor if I had listened to my grandmother's advice. But I couldn't picture myself running around with blood shouting "code blue" or "code purple." While I try to handle my health CRISIS at home, I listen to my fantasy radio to clear my head.

***

I guess Invictans are not as progressive as their neighbor... Yet?

Nueva Luna Land elected a woman as leader for the first time – The Eagle just took the leader position. A crown well deserved for her. Congratulations, and good luck!

Tomorrow, it might be The Dolfin's turn to have that "chance" and get congratulated. Invictan ladies seem to be ready for another tan-suit wearing LOTIS and take back control of their bodies. But they shouldn't put the cart before the horse; the leading contenders in the ruling race must watch their respective partners in a face-to-face debate for the first time.

The Dog and The Owl are at it in Tales City; let's see how this family feud ends.

***

Speaking of owls, we have good news from Frawn Land: the world's most prolonged treasure hunt just concluded.

No, this is not about the golden ball prize drama caused by Jokri receiving the accolade instead of Victorious, despite the latter being the People's obvious choice – a story as old as time.

You know the song; I keep myself to myself and have no opinion on this.

I don't even know who they are; I'm stuck on the rivalry between Ciriano Oraldo and Lio Massi.

Back to the hunt: I thought the Treasured Safe was buried there, but it was just a 31-year-old golden statuette of the head-spinning animal that was unearthed.

I guess Ellie and Smarties are not the only hunt lovers, as thousands (if not xillions) of people were looking for the precious prize.

It reminds me of that story from the Xieta Verse about a woman who found a mysterious rug buried in her new house garden. Not a golden *Fabroké* egg, not some pirate's stolen heart, not even a celestial body, just dirt, nothing else.

I'd say that happens with every hunt – there's always one fortunate person and many disappointed ones. But they all enjoy it; they are just cool people in a peaceful place, and that's what I love.

However, I'm still not satisfied with that rug story's outcome.

Who buries a rolled rug with nothing inside?

Wait, what if the prize is the rug? Did they even have that thing appraised? Some of those Holy Land's ancient rugs are priceless!

***

Peacefulness is a feeling I cannot duplicate in my fairytale love hunt, but maybe that's because I never asked to participate.

I tried to hang in there, but the reality was more potent, and I stopped believing in finding the prince who would save me.

Maybe one day I will feel free on a midnight ride with my zombie love.

However, as we are reaching the end of the year, I'm falling more in life than in love. I, too, wanted to invent love and be hypnotized by a good man, find someone for me, like Jane Loe keeps doing.

I used to say, "Everyone suffers, but my heart of stone can't."

I must confess that I bleed the same way. I have been doing so internally for as long as I can remember.

All this introspection made me realize I need to happily dance alone for the time being if I don't want to burst into tears on a desperate wedding day someday.

Sorry for crying out loud.

Unfortunately, it's not about love; it's about life.

My story is not that special. My whole life, I've looked at the bright side of any situation; I've been pushing through with no tears or words. I've watched people live extraordinary lives, and it always felt like I was a spectator of mine. I've never been satisfied with what I have and what I have achieved in a world obsessed with perfection.

At least I'm still alive. "Mercy me," the Universe doesn't seem to forget about me completely.

Sorry for my broken heart.

I keep apologizing because I know how people hate losers.

I'm not even sure I am one; I only know I wasn't born a winner.

I did everything right, but it never felt suitable.

Another morning, another suffocating day, but I came a long way, so I know I should shut up and play my part in society.

What am I supposed to do? What if it's quitting time? How am I supposed to pay my bills? I don't know yet, so let's rebrand it "quiet quitting."

While doing that, I figured out the right question to ask myself: "What would you do if you didn't have any bills to pay and you were already free?"

Speechless, I still don't know; my rationalist brain won't let me imagine a life where I'm not chained to my corporate job and I don't stress about bills.

***

One who doesn't have financial stress is my dear trust-funded Ellie, who has plenty of time to text me regarding Mrs. Invictana's whereabouts.

"It's so important," she says.

I didn't ask for more information, but she gave it for free: "Mrs. Invictana was spotted in a public PDA session with Wild Valentine." Great, I see they're still not beating the ghetto allegations.

The PDA is not that relevant to my cogitative brain, which prefers to remember why there was a 13 printed on the merch tote bag Ellie gifted me back in June.

For people outside Mrs. Invictana's bubble: it means thirteen years old – when she wrote and acted in her first drama play at school. That's also when she left our shared Great Banter Land's small town to reinvent herself in hopes of reaching Invictus glory.

A successful bet on her part!

I don't even think anyone knows this fun fact.

***

What was I doing at thirteen?

What were my dreams before I decided to follow my aseptic path?

I was a girl with a dual personality: self-effacing one day, the life of the party the next; always living in a fantasy world in her head.

It's a bummer I wrote none of my fantasies, whether songs or stories.

Why? I was already tired of writing essays for school; I wouldn't do that for fun! I also had other things to do, like sports events and parties, and I was mainly worried about my future.

Then, I was determined to succeed the usual way. Objectively, I'm not sure we can call it a success.

Finally, since I bagged my first job, I was left to believe that maybe one day I'll win the lottery and I'll be able to retire earlier than expected. Today, my hopeless heart stopped believing in the winning ticket that could spark a new life with surprises.

I only have one solution left: saving myself.

"Save Lady Clover, save her fantasy world, (*yatta*)!"

Hear me out, open the gate!

I will do what it takes to reach greatness and my happiness.

Do I ultimately believe in it? Like the idea of ghosts, I'm not sure, but I know I get a rush of blood when I think about it. The beauty of this self-rescue mission is that there's no defined right way to do it.

I stayed up all night trying to find an idea. One minute, it's crystal clear and unbelievable; the next, there's no good feelings, and I doubt everything.

Among a thousand crazy ideas, I chose one of my new-year resolution: write a song. Just one, it shouldn't be that complicated.

Luck seems to be on my side as I have this brilliant idea at the most wonderful time of the year: I'm on paid leave – plenty of time ahead.

In the midst of writing sessions, let's party, baby!

***

I'm not sick anymore; let's find ourselves a splendid scenery to be productive and find a theme to write about.

For the first time in my life, I arrive at the airport before the check-in even starts.

Motivation, is it you? Where were you?

I board the supersonic plane, and I have a smirk the whole time. While I'm daydreaming about my next life, I can imagine the pilots following their preflight checklist as per procedure.

I look at burning engines through the little window; we move, the speed limit reaches *X1*, no going back possible.

Take-off! We are up in the air and ready to be our own hero.

The grain of hope left in me chose row 13, pushing my luck to be seated next to my soulmate.

Guess what? The flight attendant asked me to sit on the exit row instead while boarding the plane.

I can't make this up. *Fluff* my life!

I love her hair, but that looks like jealousy! That flight attendant said I looked "fit enough to do the job in an emergency."

"Lies she tells!" I screamed in my head.

She's jealous of my future love invention, and she needs glasses!

I didn't find a way to explain why I didn't want to change seats without raising a few craziness alarms, so I agreed.

It's not the time to end up on a no-flight list; my life is about to change.

***

Touchdown, here I come: Tulips Land's Adam City, the cradle of Adamers, led by Tulip Land's Monarch, The Hare.

It's another Land with a dual ruling system similar to Great Banter Land's and Cran Land's.

* Lights, camera, action * I disembark the plane in slow motion, Wowlywood style, with the wind as the supporting role.

Does this Kenau woman who decided to stand in front of me at the baggage carousel area even know who I am? Free place all around me, but blocking my view is what *she*'s choosing?

I'm whispering, "Just breathe, Seely; with each minute that passes, you're getting closer to a private jet experience."

I took my suitcase, ordered a taxi, and checked in.

It's a friendly hotel with luxury, memory foam mattress and pillows.

Also essential, I won't have to think about what to eat.

I have one job, write a one-hit wonder and convince a singer to interpret it. Ka-ching!

***

First, I need to relax slightly after the plane seat disappointment.

I go to the rooftop's infinity pool lounge, find the perfect spot on a deckchair, and take it all in.

An enjoyable, cozy electro song is playing, and the hospitality manager comes to order my drink. I thought of tea but ordered a spicy margarita – *#Lost*.

Yum-Yum, paired with sweet cherries – orgasmic.

"Disfruto mucho."
"Muchas gracias."

Oh my, wait! Wrong foreign language. My favorite drink is always an easy distraction.

"Smakelijk eten, smakelijk drinken!"
"Echt heel erg bedankt."

The night is continuing, and I feel happier. That might be the spicy margarita's effect, or it's me, changing already and chanting frantically:

"1, 2, 3, 4, 5, 6, 7, 8... 2, 3, 4, 5, 6, 7, 8... 3, 4, 5, 6, 7, 8... 4, 5, 6, 7, 8... 5, 6, 7, 8... 6, 7, 8... 7, 8... 8"

"8... 7, 8... 6, 7, 8... 5, 6, 7, 8... 4, 5, 6, 7, 8... 3, 4, 5, 6, 7, 8... 2, 3, 4, 5, 6, 7, 8... 1, 2, 3, 4, 5, 6, 7, 8..."

"Ate! And with that, I'll take a $2^{136,279,841}$ cocktail minus one lime." I foolishly say to the bartender.

Life is good, so let's add a tasty espresso martini to the concoction. Here I am, dancing late 'cause I'm a writer! Well, songwriter would be more appropriate, but I don't care! It's so much fun!

It was an unforgettable night that ended with me drunk on the steps of my hotel, wondering if I had just understood Dreizenberg's uncertainty principle or uncovered the secret of life. Don't tell anyone, but (*whispering*) I think it's knowing that you can control your destiny any day, at any time. *The Fate You Can't Escape* is not absolute; it's just a made-up film in my head.

That's when Aarush made my chrome nails glimmer like diamonds at dawn. I hope I find my way home...

Confused, I hobble to my hotel room, close my eyes, and dive into sweet dreams.

***

I woke up with a balloon and a do-not-disturb door hanger in my face. I recognize my handwriting on the door hanger, which reads:

"Clover River."

Maybe I should stop playing and drinking. Darling, I am not okay, and I don't understand what the cryptic message means.

What if I found the perfect idea but can't remember it because of my demons? So sad.

Cold comfort, it's continental breakfast time. Then, it's time for a little nap, windmill spotting in the afternoon, happy hour drinks, dinner, party, and sleep time.

Switch the windmill discovery with a visit to the Vogh museum, the beer museum, the tulip museum, a fellow diarist's house, a cheese factory, the Cry stadium, a fun dungeon, an ice bar, a canal tour, or the red district and… repeat that for ten days.

It's the same old song; I don't know where time went.

I haven't written a single line of the Savior song; it's time to pack up my suitcase and return home.

What a good way to put a little hurt on myself.

This salvation trip is becoming my worst nightmare.

Let's forget about it all and never mention composing again.

***

A dashing Adamer tried to initiate a dialogue at the airport, but I pretended I was in a hurry. I'm not interested anymore; I'm way too enraged by myself.

He's way too lovely anyway, asking me if I needed help to close my overstuffed hand luggage after Stanlay from TSA made me open it.

If you're wondering, "No, it wasn't a pew-pew or María's gift," just my fat water bottle I kept for hydration.

Anyway, I can spot a fake when I see one – just another North Port Prince I don't have time for.

If only I knew that the plane was delayed, I would have tried it… or not.

***

I go to the duty-free zone to kill time and spend money on things I don't need. While wandering the aisles, I eavesdrop on two sales assistants' conversation about fantasy news.

"Clio! Guess who didn't win the *Noble* Peace Prize? Your work bestie!"

"Griet! It's not surprising to me; you live for drama! Who won then?"

"A group from Cherry Land – the Non-Nucleankyo proved the obvious: red pimples should be avoided and untouched at all costs to prevent permanent scars that can destroy lives."

"Are you still talking about peace, or is that another category?"

"That was peace. *Noble* Medicine Prize was awarded for marvelous progress in micro-NDA, *Noble* Physics Prize was granted for the breakthrough in coffee machine learning with artificial intelligence and..."

Clio interrupts Griet: "Let me guess, *Noble* Literature Prize was assigned to Mrs. Invictana's PTSD manuscript and *Noble* Chemistry Prize to her and Wild Valentine's love invention!"

"Girl, bye! The *Noble* Chemistry Committee honored geniuses for their innovative flavored protein shakes and the Literature prize was awarded to the well-deserved Hun Tang! Her poetic prose would end Invictan clans' rivalries and every war in the world if it could reach all affected. She grasps the ubiquitous ambivalence of trauma and ascertains the fragility of Xian existence.

Nothing compares to the pain induced by abrupt departures, especially when innocent children are at stake. It's the Rowan Empire I think about every day. I always follow my mother's advice, never to avoid saying the names of loved ones and departed people to honor their memories and remember their everlasting smiles in our hearts.

It might also be Great Banter Land's Kountess' as I heard she showed up for the devastated dance kids' family in Big Smoke City. Mournful and overflowing tears came down my face like flash floods destroying Bull Land. Tragedies overlay and my distress and impotence could only be lessened by images of Scranishs' exemplary resilience, solidarity, and pragmatism. They invented the kind of love that should be more talked about." Griet added with teary eyes.

"Damn! OK, 50-year-old colleague! Your monologue is giving Hermans! I'm struck dumb."

"Stop it. I wish I were as good as him, or I could escape from my duty incognito like Mr. Mi-Name. Have you heard he is a grandfather now? Our little niece got married in May and is now expecting! I wish I could be, too! I love babies! Damn! We're getting old."

"I believe in magic, don't panic. Maybe you should write a letter to Exron; he's at baby 17 and looking for surrogates to populate Planet X. You're a good impersonator; you can be his lonely muse."

"Well, if he can catch me the way his artificial arms are recapturing rockets, I might consider it."

"And you might be next to be indicted or jump next to The Phoenix. Your life, your rules. I trust Warwinism and Theros."

"Well, the good ones like The Brown are already taken. Homie is now bin balling with his son, Brownie. What do you want me to do?"

"Enjoy your penthouse in the sky, Machiavella of the upper class! I'll keep my painter and red wine."

Then, my nosy ears heard the airport speakers: "Last call and final call for Seely Clover, Terminal 2, boarding gate S10."

I haven't exercised in a year, and I'm expected to outrun Flo Delores Joker. My rabbit heart felt between my lungs, but I made it before take-off.

While cruising, I spot a rare Blue Morpho solitary butterfly known to live forever, flying through purple clouds, and following its own direction. It feels like an elegiac moment, and my visible sorrow attest to it.

***

I landed safely, and I am thankful I avoided a "Pull up, terrain!"
episode.

Back home, looking at the fog, I conclude that swimming days are
over, and Sunshine and blue skies are gone. All I imagined as light is
now heavier than ever, and my smile slowly evaporates.

My exit from the plane is not as glorious as my arrival in Tulip
Land.

At the airport, I take the new Exron self-flying cab, and I have a
smooth journey until it ejects me on the corner of Camelia Street.

My bruises and ripped clothes make me perfectly blend into the
crowd of shapeshifters, skeletons, zombies, robots, witches, giant
worms, Deluwood cosplays, or green ogre ladies and lords.

I had forgotten Willoween scares and "tricks-and-treaties" night.

I remember the last Willoween I enjoyed, but it didn't end well.

A few years ago, I pledged not to take part in any anime cosplay
frenzy or role play as there's a risk my innocent, fully-dressed photos
might be leaked in a revenge smut campaign, the way Exron released
Chamber Hurt's pics. I hope the poor woman is finally enjoying a
peaceful life. I feel for her and every lady who fell into that easy love
trap – again, learning more from strange behavioral patterns and people's mistakes. I'm welcoming everyone in the learning curve.

Anyway, I walk home, head tilted to the side, my heels' sound
echoing on Camelia Street, one step at a time.

On my way home, I call my lawyer, Analyze Keystone, to see if what just happened could be a defective vehicle lawsuit that would get me fair physical and psychological compensation.

She hung up – connection issues.

***

Time flies, and I am home.

I'm spiraling and at the far edge of what some people end up calling a sewerslide. I'm saddled with doubts and fears, feeling as stuck as those astronauts stranded in Planet X's orbit, but I know I don't want to wear Beanie Haylish's necklace.

So, what if I work to become the best version of myself, regain confidence, and go to the Andromeda galaxy if it still doesn't work here on Planet X?

If I leave, will I ever come back? Will it be the last time I see people I love, or is there a secret garden where we always meet?

I can't bet on that. Hence, I won't abandon ship.

Let's create a random remixed idiom: "Sticks and stones may break my bones, but they'll never break my soul."

***

Even crystal ball aficionados notice that something's not right, energetically speaking. And we all know that a shift in planets' alignment can mess up translations and moods. Or maybe that's a modern society's issue – too much unnecessary deep analysis.

Can a negative mind give you a positive life?

My grandmother used to say: "If you look long enough for a problem you hadn't noticed, you might end up finding a made-up one."

It feels off, but I still have hope that one day, I will enjoy a blinding cosmic love and my hometown scenery.

Maybe today's the day. Here I go, sitting on the back porch with a plaid on my lap, contemplating leaves falling from the tree and listening to birds chirping while drinking a pumpkin chai tea.

It might be enough for me, simple pleasures.

In the meantime, here I am... still sinking.

11

November

Here we are... celebrating.

November fever, forever!

Let's put my dream hunt aside, the same way I usually skip this month because I'm so impatient to reach the end of the year and see what's on the other side that I forget to appreciate its beauty.

I might not be able to seize the day, but the crisp air and the sound of my steps in my frost-bitten garden warm my Xian heart.

A sense of overwhelming gratitude flourishes when you're reminded of your fleeting existence. Maybe that's why I am as present as Hai Trinat on his streaming pentathlon on the Xieta Verse in November XX24.

***

I, too, want to celebrate my 100th anniversary one day like The Harrier – an exceptional milestone reached by the adored former Invictus Land leader.

It would still be necessary that our lives don't end up at risk with the outcome of the current ruling race. Do we even realize what's happening?

No distractions are allowed when the future of Invictus Land and the world is at stake. And I never exaggerate the reality of any situation. Maybe this world where nobody truly lives will catch fire, and it's a lost cause – but I still choose to think otherwise, even if the ghost of my doubts makes me suffer inside.

Two candidates, two methods; I need to get closer to action.

***

Let's find ourselves a suitable scenery.

Here I come, Chocolate City – the First City of Invictus Land.

Willi Winkatt should have opened a chocolate factory here to help Invictans cope with all the stress his predictions caused.

As he didn't, I will try a half-smoke with Mambo sauce or a Cheesepick Bay blue crab. I'll burn the corresponding calories next year. There is no time for a jog by the Podomat River with Gazelle Brilliant, Robin Deaton, and the Petite Dame; I have visits planned.

***

I start with the Invictus Mall park and its obelisk.

I almost got scared that my plane had dropped me back to Gifted Land as the obelisk style is reminiscent of theirs. I told you; all roads lead back to Mother Land.

I wander the breathtaking park and stop by the Agram L. Cole Memorial. I feel so small in front of the majestic stone statue.

He's Invictus greatness at its best: "In this house, as in the hearts of Invictans for whom he rescued the Unity, the remembrance of Agram L. Cole is preserved infinitely."

Among his most significant achievements, the late Agram L. Cole has issued the *Emancipation Treaty* and helped write the 13th law.

For those who need a reminder, in a not-so-old past, all Xians were not equal on Planet X. Abominable times punctuated with dreadful plantations, appalling weeping trees, and indelible inequities. With the *Emancipation Treaty*, slavery of the oppressed people was abolished.

To my surprise, talking to the locals, I discovered that the abhorrent times are not entirely in the past.

While listening to Rev. Hal Sharpman in the museum, I understand that the chronic wound of the segregated Invictus Land's history can't heal as it keeps reopening because of trauma and burns.

While descending the stairs on my way out of the memorial, I noticed a few words engraved on one step. I read it out loud: "I HAVE A FANTASY. Martyn L. Keen Jr. The demonstration on Chocolate City for jobs and freedom. Chapter 8 X8 XX63."

A little girl skipping down the stairs overheard that, turned back, and said to me: "He who died for their sins." She left running and giggling. She was a perfect example of innocence and pure joy.

I wish I knew what I should do to feel free. I don't recall those years of unclouded happiness. I am not even sure I could ever experience it.

I asked; my family says I did. Age devours our memories and recollections do vary. Only exceptional historical events remain untouched, undebatable, and remembered in all the same way.

"I have a fantasy" speech is one of those rare treasures. A century later, we can still hear these powerful words echoing in streets filled with Invictans from all backgrounds. It's almost as if I was there and here simultaneously, living a dream come true of an assembled multitude fighting for equal rights.

Why can't worldwide descendants of oppressors understand they should break the hurt cycle? Is it that complicated to be Xian and act with basic decency?

Maybe I should have added that as a wish to the genie in the bottle.

Considering that Holy Land conflicts are escalating and Planet X is still not at peace, I bet it wouldn't have changed anything. But at least I would have tried.

***

Just like Invictans tried to help Blue Dragon Land's southern allies take over the North of Blue Dragon Land for 20 years (IX55-IX75) but unexpectedly failed against the Bluedramese local warriors, also known as 'Blue Gongs.'

To further understand this ancient conflict from Region IV (+; −), I spent the next day in the Bluedramese veterans' memorial, where you can see names of fallen lives.

Even after a deeply reflective day, it's still unclear whether Invictans were trying to save Bluedramese from Red Dragon Land's influence or cage them for their own gain. The Longhorn, Invictus' leader at the time, gave flawed justifications for his war launch.

Invictan soldiers went from "hell yeah, a little affray" to "hell no, we won't go," and the public, alarmed by the devastation and the violence of this war, gradually joined protests.

Maybe The Longhorn should have asked a native Taler for advice, as minding his own business would have saved over 58,000 Invictan lives and xillions of victims among Blue Dragon Land and its neighboring countries. There were fewer casualties on Invictus Land's side, but they still lost the battle against Blue Gongs' strategies, their jungle, heat, and mosquitoes.

Who would have thought that bigger guns wouldn't necessarily secure the win for Invictus Land? A tiny dragonfly flew by and whispered in my ear: "Well, little old me."

That said, when you look closer, it gets more apparent that they shouldn't have started this fight in the first place.

I even found a striking similarity between both past adversaries. One side is wearing tin foil hats to avoid their minds being controlled by leaders or Aliens; the other side is wearing an innovative biodegradable conical hat made with leaves, bamboo, or reeds – protection against electromagnetic waves and paranormal encounters vs. protection against heat and rain. Everybody wants to be protected, seen and loved – same old, same old.

Maybe even as old as the ancient legend of *A* Goddess descending from the sky during an unprecedented downpour that caused significant damage throughout Blue Dragon Land. That Goddess wore an alluring conical hat woven with cosmic leaves and bamboo sticks that protected the whole Land and its people. The Goddess has taught them how to raise crops like rice and live harmoniously with nature.

Reassured and peaceful at dusk on her last day there, Bluedramese fell asleep to *A* Goddess' chants. They regained their consciousness with sunshine emerging, but *A Goddess* was already gone, and her story is now fading with time like ancient ciphers engraved in Gifted Land's temples. That's not a good way to say goodbye, but it adds to the beauty of the myth.

***

I brought a pretty bouquet of purple irises to leave by the dedicated wall at the Bluedramese Women's Memorial, but a rude woman named Karen told me that only red, blue, or white roses were appropriate for the occasion, and she threw my flowers away.

I'm a pacific girl who doesn't like conflict, especially in sacred or commemorative places, so I rushed out of there, head down.

Beating the clock out of a place you want to explore because of a flower gate is so XX24 coded.

Why did I even choose purple irises when Ellie suggested I should bring lillies? I thought she was teasing me with that play on words, but now I figured she was right.

My left brain also kept screaming poppies, and I disregarded them because they're my all-time favorites, and the probability it would fit the occasion was close to 0.001%. That's a standard error Nekeyah, or Calseeya would have computed better. They can solve any problem.

It doesn't even matter. That Karen is not worth my time or energy; let's forget about her.

I should leave that and my avoidance coping behind. I can't wait to get through the new year gate and overcome my indecisiveness.

***

If I had more hours to explore these amazing memorials, I would have also gotten deeper into the myths originating from Calm Land (+; +). Calm Land is the once united cradle of Calmeans, but now divided into two parts – led by The Lynx Dynasty in the north and The Tiger in the south. The northern part, also known as Calm Night Land, is one of the most powerful and mysterious Lands on Planet X. The Lynx is a feared but respected man of few words, just like his friend The Libra. The southern part, also known as Calm Morning Land, is mostly known for its vibrant culture that is trending worldwide. From C-Pop to C-Drama, Calmeans are all resplendent!

Alas, I couldn't stop by the charcoal statues stuck in time to know more about Calm Land as I tried to prevent Karen from spewing hate at me for another insane reason.

These statues struck me like thunderlight; it felt like looking at me, seemingly in movement but always mired in the past and my regrets.

***

It's a new day with a new mood. Luckily, today, I have bigger fish to fry, and I'm being told The Phoenix is looking for the adversary within while visiting Chocolate City and serving Frawnch fries at Big Monald.

Yes, you heard me right. It has nothing to do with April's 'Take Your Child to Work Day' at *Los Rojos Hermanos*. The Phoenix is living his blue-collar dream, and he enjoys it. I would have passed by to grab some fries with my fish if my hysterical friend Jeffrey Signfelt hadn't opted for a coffee-tasting experience instead.

Jeffrey is that kind of friend you only see every five years but who's always there in spirit. Curiously, when we reconnect, it never feels like we ever lost touch.

Jeffrey picks me up in the morning with a fancy car from the IX60s. We try coffee in three different places at Invictus Mall, and none seem to please him. He then offered to accompany me on a guided visit to the ILHM Museum, as his expertise in the subject would help me gain more insight into some historical aspects.

Trigger warnings for sensitive souls: this is a poignant experience but necessary. This museum is dedicated to sparking conversations about delicate themes like genocide, hatred, dignity, freedom, and democracy.

Making an analogy with toasts given at both family parties on the *SYTYCR* show, I realize some fights will take several generations or even a planet's lifetime to resolve. I guess the most important thing is never giving up.

Filled with vexed emotions, Jeffrey and I leave the museum and head to Cherry Trees Park next to Invictus Mall.

It's the closest I've been to Cherry Land, a place I would love to visit one day. The last time I tried, I booked a ticket, got stuck in translation, and ended up in Sunburnt Land – part of the *Seldom Wealth Treaty*, led by His Highness The Unicorn and represented by the local Optimister – The Koala.

I was glad to hear it's a place where the Xieta Verse has been banned for children under sixteen. Then, long story short, all my phobias kicked in, and I fainted when I realized the plane had landed in the cradle of Sunburtians (or affectionately Sunnies).

They all seemed nice, but I boarded the next plane back home.

If you want to mention sharks, giant spiders, killer coconuts, or bodybuilding kangaroos... just delete me here, decrease me, crop me from the picture, and leave me alone.

Real PTSD, don't ask me anything about Sunburnt Land; ask the Hems family, Marjo Ruby, Katie Freegirl, Huge Jackguy, Rylie Nirogue, or Nichold Childman.

***

I fear I may have nightmares now; maybe I should ask The Dolphin, who just arrived in Chocolate City, to light a candle for me at the church she's visiting.

After a second thought, I wouldn't make any holy requests, as I remember my grandmother always telling me never to ask sky beings for favors, only for forgiveness. I can admit my grandmother's advice could sometimes be uncommon and outdated. That said, with complete objectivity, no one on Planet X could even come close to her wisdom. I said what I said.

Back to The Dolphin, who wants "all souls to vote for the greater good and have compassion." She urges everyone to try a little tenderness, become peacemakers, spread joy around, choose light over darkness, and be inspired by every day Good Samaritans.

She promises her leadership will be just, undivided, and stable.

However, she fears Los Rojos' ruling might bring chaos and loathing. Everybody in attendance at the local church agrees with her.

The only thing left to do is convince outsiders.

To do so, The Dolphin must leave Chocolate City now to travel across Invictus Land and meet people.

One of her memorable stops is in Invictus' Jumbo City.

Everything's bigger in Jumbo City: beeves, cows, trucks, roads, boots, hats, people, and their egos. No, the latter has not been proven yet. But when it matters, natives of Jumbo City show up, no questions asked. That's why The Dolphin organizes a little get-together there or, should I say, a high-end bottomless brunch.

The "who's who" of "get that" is there – among them, Queen V with her mom Thena, her sister Ketty, and all her family.

The vibrant brunch opening toast is given by Ketty, who's sporting an oversize androgynist commander look while explaining she's down for whatever The Dolphin offers. Her motivation is clear; she will not tolerate misogyny, hatred, division, racism, or any control over her *body*. Just like me, she seems tired of people controlling her narrative. She's ready to help The Dolphin build a loving community, "grab the pen," and write a new Invictus story filled with hope, strength, and equality.

Then love takes over Queen V's motherly heart, and she joins her sister for a toast. It's always weird to see Queen V in flesh and bone, out of a movie screen. Even in her pajamas, she's demure, so of course, seeing her with a short neon dress – giving us the corporate look I never managed to pull, she's dazzling. She's not one to appear in public if it's not essential; as she explains, she's attending the brunch for "unity, positivity, and freedom." She gives an air kiss to the brunch attendees and exits the venue, just after hinting at a new movie release.

Following her for the next toast is her friend, Mrs. Invictana, wearing Haili's floating boohoo blue dress. She's on break from her *Auras* and sold on the bottomless concept.

I'm in no position to judge her appeal for the drink. The Phoenix might be, as he's allegedly deciding to spew hate at her for no reason – not only that, but he is also allegedly using deepfakes to convince Smarties she's supporting him.

Her presence can be seen as a statement to counterattack misinformation spread. She might also be here to warn whoever thinks they can offer to "give her a child and babysit her cats" of a great war to come. She then encourages Smarties to enter the chat, and we all know that when she speaks, they listen, and the votes swing. At the end of her speech, she reads a pleasing extract from one of her plays: "My BODY, my decision, my love."

Then, the smitten Wild Valentine barges into the venue, lifts Mrs. Invictana, and cradles her in his arms to protect her while exiting. They will never let you forget they are certified love inventors, like ever.

Finally, Robean gets up and takes the mic to toast because she can do whatever she wants. Dressed to impress with a mahogany leather ensemble and rocking her short silver curls, the unapologetic Triangulum Islands native tells the DJ not to stop the music for her speech, as she enjoys the background sound.

She starts by taking a bow to The Dolphin, who's hosting the fantastic brunch, and then she goes on with a never-ending speech about not being able to vote for *SYTYCR* herself but urging Invictans to fight for their rights in these complicated times they're facing. She fears "no love will be allowed" if The Phoenix wins.

What's bred in the bone will come out in the flesh; the party girl hypes up all attendees, asks bartenders to pour all glasses, and cheers to The Dolphin's success. Everybody drinks to that, and they dance until the music of the sun goes down.

The party ends, and Robean is seen arguing with anti-love people on her way home. The grapevine relates that these troublemakers wandered in the streets when they overheard her private joke about using her son's ID to enter a nightclub. Bad girl gone good had them forgotten how she used to be.

I wish I were there to witness her clapbacks so I could use it next time I meet another Karen. I would have watched and learned how to talk that talk on the spot. Every time someone is trying to get under my skin and disrespect me, I'm in a rare jovial mood or in the middle of a dissociative phase, and I am bereft of speech. The good part is that I'm numb to attacks; I just need to drag the words out of my mouth and let the belligerent person know I am not one to mess with.

***

A few days have passed, and word on the street is that most women "understand the assignment" and will tread on the heels of The Dolphin, Queen V, Mrs. Invictana, and Robean.

The rest seem to be in a quandary about who will best serve their interests and who they should trust. Some even express a kind of celebrity fatigue, calling into question their legitimacy to tell people what vote they should make.

Debates get crazier by the minute, and conspiracy theories are at their highest high when D-Day comes.

Time stops, and I am interrupted on my next visit.

We can hear a pin drop in Chocolate City as we get to November's bummock: Invictus Land's *SYTYCR* results.

Remembering the last leader's unveiling 5 years ago, I expected a week-long drummer roll and unsustainable suspense.

Nothing of the kind – the result is announced in the twinkling of an eye.

And the winner is... about to be revealed, and a change is going to come.

Invictans start swinging and rocking in anticipation of the results.

Fortune tellers, experts in all fields, commentators, and self-proclaimed analysts expect The Dolphin to win.

***

The Phoenix.

It's... The Phoenix.

It's The Phoenix.

Here he is, claiming victory at breakneck pace.

He declares it's him before *SYTYCR* officials do.

It's The Phoenix. He won.

When you exude confidence and know your worth, you plan the winning celebrations accordingly.

The Phoenix did, does, and always will.

He toasts: "the best family of all time and the beginning of Invictus' Diamond Age."

Sorry, the emotional rollercoaster and the abrupt divulging made me forget my etiquette classes.

I want to congratulate the voted winner, The Phoenix.

Many bubbles just popped, and people who doubted his popularity were proved wrong. His promises to solve territorial and economic problems were music to most Invictans' ears. But he wants to calm everyone as he pledges to fix it all.

Proud of his remarkable comeback as Invictus Land's leader and happy with The Owl's incentive, he also takes the occasion to thank

Exron, the unexpected rising star in the ultimate moments of *SYTY-CR*, who strongly believes "Invictus is under attack."

The Phoenix has a dream of making Invictus Land healthy, wealthy, and happy again. Please don't make him lose this dream. He takes his almost resurrection as a sign from above for him to take the lead and change lives forever. Who am I for not believing this might be another case of *A* God apparition? No one.

I've been told that my biggest fault is being too optimistic and naive. Whether or not true, I only see one option: respect people's votes and join forces for the greater good. I'm willing to accept a V. for Victory, not for Vendetta. If you ask my predictions for his term, I think it will be alright. I would even add that it will start in XX25, the last perfect square year of this century! I know it's the year of the alleged project XX25, too, but my bank teller Tamra J. Handsome's predictions might be wrong, and The Phoenix won't do all the crazy things he's rumored to have planned.

I can picture him improving Invictan health access, fixing consumer goods prices, and spreading love worldwide while not forgetting to celebrate each win with his signature dance move. Look how happy he is with his *SYTYCR* win! Happy people don't do bad things, right?

I put all my trust in him to do the best possible for Invictus Land and the world.

You can take Seely out of empathy, but you can't take the empath out of Seely.

***

It is now officially confirmed that The Phoenix is the winner. It means no more hope for his opponent. The thrill is gone for Los Blaus family.

It's another proof that good girls usually finish last. My empathy is now flooding, and The Dolphin is nowhere to be seen. Even if her deserted party venue is a broken reflection of abandoned malls across Invictus Land, she remains a Legend for her supporters.

She fought like a Gladiator, and that deserves respect. Some say she was late to bloom; others consider she was dealt an intricate hand from the start. Helped with an unlimited budget and influential people, she still chose joy and peace.

The Dolfin won't be the one singing the Invictus Symphony theme next year, but she stayed true to her values.

Her family, friends, and supporters who voted for her are drowning in their own tears. Stuck in an apparent bubble of people who truly understood the assignment, they had a vision of her peacefully taking care of business.

I wonder what happened to that solidarity. I hope everyone finds the strength to fill their void and survive through the feared storms ahead. If they don't have it in them, my only advice would be to channel someone else's.

They say, "Practice what you preach." I faced a difficult situation at work, and I found the strength to speak up in the inspiring "Ka Mate" of The White Cloud Land's native representatives fighting for their rights. Did it work? No, but at least I tried.

There's not a dry eye in Chocolate City, but because of my self-diagnosed familial dysautonomia, I can't cry with them, unfortunately. Maybe I should ask my friend Tirease to lend me some tears for the day. Am I blue? Yes, I am because it's heartbreaking to witness dreams and hopes destroyed.

I am just left wanting... MORE! More time, more work, more knowledge, more... representation. I hate it when I can't get rid of 'What Ifs' or 'Maybes' in my head, and my overthinking reaches uncontrollable levels. Usually, this is when my left brain takes back control and shuts it all down – it shifts my perspective to ensure it's in charge.

Have I been brainwashed about how great The Dolphin was, or is it all authentic and objective? Had a Rogue Ane podcast appearance would have helped secure the leader prize?

Last month, we learned that it's important not to focus on your opponent to win the musical chairs. So, instead of offering an alternative to The Phoenix's dance, it may have been necessary to add more depth and Substance to win more hearts.

But if we compute the probability of her winning in all neutrality and considering all vectors, what were The Dolphin's chances?

Will Invictus Land ever be ready for a Female Sage?

Will Rose ever beat Wayne? Not sure...

Blau family supporters doubt it, and some Invictans already plan to move abroad. From $\xi 1$ houses advertised in Italic Land to a life off-grid in Triangulum Islands, their dreams are unrestricted if and only if they are far away from The Phoenix.

Panic will cloud anyone's judgment, and even the most brilliant people will make mistakes when befuddled by their ideas of the good, the bad, and the dirty. Invictans, inspired by Chocolate City's aerospace museum, even consider defying gravity and flying to the Moon, Saturn, or Messier 13 globular cluster.

Let's hope they don't get stuck in orbit because of another Blooming malfunction, like astronauts Summita Wellams and Berry Gilmore.

Should I also tell them they'll need Exron's help for that one? Maybe I should wait a little longer – unless they use the innovative wooden satellite launched from Cherry Land. I already know the pigtails Vikeen girl would sign for that option and the COPE92's new ξ300 zillion climate deal.

***

While Invictans are choosing their next pied-à-terre, I think about visiting the emblematic Off-White House before I leave.

Unfortunately, I can't even get close enough to take a picture as the place is highly crowded. I hear on the bush telegraph that some heretics and egomaniacs are brandishing guns, singing war songs, and blocking access to the emblematic monument. I usually want to see things with my own eyes to believe it, but this time, I chose not to bother.

That will be the day I won't even try to use a drone for an aerial view. They might throw mud at it like angry Scranishs did to protest His Majesty The Bull, who they believe didn't help enough after the flood disaster. I'm as out as Radale Naval, who is retiring from his racket life for good. I'm going to burn rubber and go back home to my cocoon. Bye, Chocolate City, it was a pleasure.

Note to self: Even a broken arrow can pierce and shatter peace. Peace is fragile.

My hometown is boring and seemingly far from any conflict, and even I expect the worst and know everything can change in a fraction of a second.

Even if you want to live your life unbothered by things out of your control, the Xieta Verse will never let you.

I continue my little routine, boiling with a stress I can't expose in a world led by bros. I'm so irritable, and everybody should know!

***

I find refuge in laughter and silly stories like the continuing feud between Startstruck rivals.

Everybody thought we were on the verge of a truce between the two, but The Llama is not backing down and resumes to squabble with The Dromedary.

Pumped up by his recent announcement as the next Chef of the Super Masked Ball, The Llama preps for the main dish: a roast beef with wholegrain mustard. He shares the step-by-step recipe on a TV cooking show with whoever is interested.

It's always nice to see him in his element. Cooking is in his blood, in his DNA. Even if he takes great pride in his work, he's always humble, a good example of the Generation X he represents. The recipe for disaster has been partly concocted by Chef Antonio.

***

The steps are the following:

Step 1: Preheat oven to 200 degrees.

Lightly grease a roasting pan.

Mix onions, herbs, oil, and MUSTARD in a bowl.

Season to your liking with garlic, salt, and pepper.

Step 2: Place a piece of Wagyu beef in the center of the pan.

Spread the mixture on top.

Roast for 1 hour and 13 minutes if you prefer your beef medium rare, and more if you like it well done.

People with sensitive taste buds can add a nut of mustard to the side afterward, and those who are completely immune to it can push it and add even more MUSTARD!

Step 3: Remove the pan from the oven and slice it after 13 minutes of cooling down.

Step 4: For the healthy bunch, add two tablespoons of extra virgin oil to a mixed vegetable medley on a wok pan and sauté the mix for 6 minutes. For the carpe diem bunch, fries to the side.

Step 5: Choose a fancy plate.

Place a beef slice in the center.

Delicately lay a golden leaf on it.

Meticulously add the vegetable medley.

Add a trail of sauce to your liking.

And here you have a "*doper* than dope" dish.

Or at least that's what I thought.

Still bitter from the Starstrucks feud, The Dromedary has allegedly sought legal advice that culminated with an unfair competition lawsuit against the principal shareholders of Starstrucks, who he believes used cooking robots and favored The Llama's recipes book distribution. His lawyer – Helene Breadloft, advised him to launch a defamation lawsuit against The Llama for alleging that he's using extra virgin milk.

Everybody is confused because a lawsuit in the cooking industry has never been heard of. They say "innocent until proven guilty," so, no one can condemn the amazing Llama or Starstrucks' influential shareholders for now. But "law is law;" if the defendants did The Dromedary wrong, they must be sentenced accordingly. In the meantime, I will read every cookbook and enjoy every cook show.

***

They sure will come in handy as we get closer to the Thankshanding holiday. Thankshanding is an annual Invictan holiday celebrated every third Wednesday of November to commemorate an ancient harvest festival, give thanks, and express gratitude. My family follows the tradition since my aunt Joan married an Invictan man.

Fun fact: Invictus Land's leader officially pardons a chosen Invictan turkey every year. Experts on the matter can't agree on who started this tradition, but the majority is convinced it comes from a true man who led Invictus eighty years ago.

After The Llama's cooking show, my channel surfing got me by coincidence to watch that ceremony live.

In front of an entertained crowd, The Turtle does not break with the funny tradition this year and proceeds to pardon not once but three turkeys named Pitch, Folsom, and Huntsman. For vegan Vivians and worried Waverlys, I assure you the sublime turkeys are expected to live a happy farm life, and none of them will end up on anyone's banquet.

***

Clover Family Reunion.

I must pretend I want to cook, so I hit replay on The Llama's cooking show. I consider trying his roast beef recipe for Thankshanding Eve, but before I have time to write it down, my nephew Chad jumps on the couch, inadvertently presses the wrong button on the remote, and turns the TV off.

Chad is my sister Olivia's son. He's the cutest, but such an attention seeker, and I'm such a people pleaser who indulges in his every whim. He wants to play peekaboo and then hopscotch, and I want to continue my cooking show, but I give in because family comes first.

Olivia tells me she's going to cook anyway; she'd rather have me babysit her son than "poison" the whole family with my attempt at cooking. I won't beg her for that one! I still consider myself a 52-year-old child, so spending the afternoon playing with kids instead of cooking with adults will never annoy me.

My rich aunt Amelia is hosting us all in her mountain home.
Let the family gathering be joyful and peaceful this time around.

Last year, my two-faced aunt Joan was ranting about *SYTYCR*, calling everyone lunatics and stupid. It went from zero to a hundred, and even I was ready to cut the peace bridge.

Considering how we were over each other, I didn't expect anyone to show up this year, let alone almost everyone.

It's not the right weather for a cookout, so we can enjoy the beautifully decorated indoors with fairy light curtains, white candles, pumpkins, philamot leaves, and pinecones. The glamorous long table is ornated with foliage-themed centerpieces, plates, and cutlery. Table setting is an art. It smells like pumpkin pie spice and delicious food.

As I already knew I would be exempt from cooking, I brought drinks; that's my lane. I found unpronounceable Chateaux for the wines and a refined Frawnch sparkling wine that will divinely pair my family's talents: Aunt Amelia's crispy roast turkey, Uncle Daniel's seafood boil, my cousin Michael's grilled potatoes, Aunt Joan's green bean casserole, her decoy husband's fish crumble, my cousin Rebeka's smashed sweet potatoes, my sister Olivia's roast beef with cranberry sauce, her husband Lucas' unseasoned potato salad with raisins, my brother Levi's peas soup, his girlfriend's bear hands, and Mama Rosalyn's special touch for dessert. My dad doesn't cook but my mom's signature dessert counts for two. It's a mouth-watering apple pecan pie with luscious apples from the secret orchard in her garden. I'll try to find the recipe or ask Levi to blow the gaff.

What we won't be cooking for our Thankshanding dinner is a ξ6.2 xillion banana. That one is ART, sacred, duct-taped on the whacked-out garage wall it belongs to.

XX24 is the year of big dreams. I'm inspired and can't wait to share MY ART with the world.

I guess it's not entirely wrong that time heals all wounds. My mom says it's the power and gift of love.

This year, everyone agrees not to go anywhere close to *SYTYCR*.

My little nephew Chad wants to toast: "I want to express my gratitude to these beautiful people I call family. We are all God's children, breathing and living thanks to our heart of gold beating. I live for your love. I wish you all a xillion blessings. Unlike my classmates, I don't need superpowers as I already get them from the support each of you gives me. Please never forget what matters and never give up on us; never give up on me. I know I'm only on this planet for four long years, but I'm an old soul who exhorts you to follow your dreams. You would be surprised by the impact even small changes can make. *Ain't* no mountain high enough, *ain't* no dream big enough, *ain't* no fantasy crazy enough. Give me a Hallelujah!"

I'm not crying, you are. I'm so sensitive to children's innocence.

I can't answer back, as I'm just trying to swallow my tears.

As usual, my cousin Rebeka ruins it and interjects with: "not everybody's religious, I believe in science, you better respect my beliefs, little drummer boy."

Thankshanding XX24 is about to turn into a scary movie. Cutting Olivia's son when he's doing nothing but spreading love and wisdom was a big mistake. Hands are unionizing, and dishes are flying. No one does it better than Olivia when somebody's getting on her nerves.

I can't with this *fit* show, it's all wrong, but it's alright.

Astrologists would define Olivia as a "Libra Sun with Pisces Rising," so I don't understand where she gets her fighting spirit from.

Like me, she spent her whole life in fancy suburbs and private schools, but she's what Earthlings would call "an Aquarius born with a ghetto soul."

My scientific cousin Rebeka is now fighting for her life in paradise. No, she's not. She's lucky the scene didn't occur in an elevator; she wouldn't be here anymore to tell this story.

Oh, holiday night is turning into a silent night.

Nothing new. It's a futile cause at this point.

Sometimes, I fear I'm the last leaf on the family tree, the only one who remembers my grandmother's wisdom idioms and quotes.

I will continue to believe that hope is not lost for our family and planet as even Holy Land agrees to a ceasefire.

In the meantime, here I am... still celebrating.

12

December

HERE WE ARE... LISTENING.

In December, we listen, and we don't judge.

Hello, lack of sunshine and vitamin D deficiency!

I can sense magic in the air; that's why some Xians believe it's the best time of the year.

Who else may benefit from fairy lights and magic spells?

The Turtle's son!

One swallow doesn't make a baby; I made a mistake. The Turtle pardoned two turkeys last month, not three. My wine tasting during the Thankshanding dinner may have played a trick on my brain.

Folsom is indeed not a turkey but The Turtle's son. I watched it back, and I can see it now: the third animal is a man dressed up as a turkey. Folsom was doing a prank on his dad for his last turkey pardoning before he gave the baton to his successor, The Phoenix.

After watching that replay, I continue with live news.

The news anchor is announcing that The Turtle is pardoning his son Folsom from two convictions, sparing him any prison blues for the future. If you are confused right now, welcome to the club.

No, it's not a prank or a misunderstanding this time; it's real news. Folsom is pardoned by The Turtle, who considers those convictions "a witch hunt" to begin with – no need for a debate or judgment here. Folsom is pardoned and will not suffer any hypothetical future retaliation from The Phoenix and Los Rojos. Get over it.

***

What else should I get over with?

The Tiger, Calm Morning Land leader, declared martial arts lessons mandatory for all southern Calmeans. I unwillingly received that information from the Xieta Verse. My recent introduction to Calm Land at the memorial in Chocolate City may have inspired my algorithm because I've never had the chance to visit that Land, and I still know little about their customs. If I understood correctly, The Tiger feared political interference, and a coup orchestrated by The Lynx, his frenemy leader from Calm Night Land.

I'm not sure I can objectively link The Tiger's fear of a coup to that law aimed at implementing martial arts for all. Maybe it would help people defend themselves from any attack. I don't know, and it seems I won't have to, as Calmeans and other ruling entities quickly overturned this law. After examining it, Calmeans dubbed it a "self-coup by The Tiger," considering it wasn't just about martial arts lessons

as alleged reports of the suppression of free press and political opponents' arrests emerged. Witnessing the people's protest working to
improve lives is rare – The Tiger is impeached, arrested, and indicted.
Calmeans' quick action may have saved their peace, or if The Tiger
had been right all along, it might have helped their demise.

Time will tell.

***

Time will also tell if the ceasefire will last in Holy Land and if the death
toll count will finally stop at the reported 50,000 casualties.

Speaking of Holy Land, the world wonders if The Ibis, the Near
East region leader, will be found one day. Maybe frightened to suffer
the same fate as The Tiger and inspired by Rivers Land's Optimister's
escape plan in August, he fled his territory after rebels seized control.

The Ibis and his family had controversially ruled the Near East
part of Holy Land for a century before its inhabitants, the Neareans,
decided to depose him.

The Rebels' leader, whose name is still unknown as I write, ensures
their Land is now free and protected.

As I struggle to sleep, I watch every video suggested on the Xieta
Verse showcasing this revolution.

As they storm the abandoned palace, Neareans are flabbergasted at
the luxurious life The Ibis lived while some were starving.

It's a building storming I can watch without hurting too much.

Interviewed Neareans all report the same thing: The Ibis allegedly
left a garage full of luxury cars, among other valuable items.

While the looted palace is being explored, Neareans finally receive information about their former leader's whereabouts; he's in Golden Eagle Land, one of his longstanding allies.

The Libra shows again he is a loyal friend, as he welcomes The Ibis with open arms in his powerful Land.

***

Guess who else is welcoming leaders with open arms? The Bulldog, Frawn Land leader who couldn't be more unbothered by crazy allegations about his love life. Supported by his wife, The Chihuahua, he is doing what he excels at: throwing lavish parties.

I had my first Frawnch extravaganza introduction during the Olyxiads he hosted in July.

This time, the ceremony has a more serious tone as it's celebrating the reopening of Love-Dame Cathedral.

Amongst attendees, I notice The Killdeer – Border Land leader, who is rocking his camouflage attire to ensure no one notices him in the black-tie event. Or his cheap choice is a symbol of resistance that he may only decide to change as soon as a truce is called.

The former clown turned leader is so proud and humble, always making sure the world knows he's no different from wondrous Ureignans fighting for their beautiful Land.

This conflict against Golden Eagle Land impacted both soldiers and civilians. Casualties also approximately amount to 50,000 fallen souls while 400,000 people were injured. I bet even the heroic ladies known as 'emissaries of war' wouldn't have helped turn this situation around.

Listening to people questioning The Killdeer's risk-taking fight, I realized I was born cautious, so I would never have had the courage to pursue that. I guess only people who have to fight for freedom could understand.

Anyway, The Bulldog has other more influential personalities in his guest list, including Invictan First Lady (The Turtle's wife), The Phoenix, His Grace The Kount of GB Land, Exron, and the "who's who" of "worth what?" of the world.

The deep notes played on the organ pipes by the resurrected David John won't open the Treasured Safe, but it might open the cursed dark chest. Maybe the latter is responsible for the Frawnch cathedral catching fire five years ago.

As of now, the cause is unknown, and there are many theories that the ignition came from high-tech cigarettes left inadvertently by scaffolding robot workers, a short circuit in the electrical system, or, more unlikely, terrorism. The most probable is the first one, but the cause didn't matter when it came to raising almost ξ1 zillion in a day.

I am teary-eyed when I see the world reuniting for a noble cause. I hope the next one will be "all together against hunger."

***

Before that happens, at least we have Frawn Land and ladies worldwide supporting The Pelican. Everybody is still in shock about this lawsuit case as we are on the eve of the sentencing.

On the final court day, pounding her gavel, the judge announces, "Life imprisonment without parole, and you are lucky the plaintiff's lawyers couldn't prove sorcery and debauchery without a reasonable doubt, or you would have ended up like Joan of Arc."

The court audience applauds and cheers until the judge asks for "silence" to give notice of the remaining sentencing.

Every accomplice to the vile husband each only got 100-year of solitary confinement, and those who lied about not knowing what they were doing got 200-year imprisonment sentence as perjury in the matter is highly condemned.

After the verdict, her Honor concludes, and The Pelican exits the court, hoping her courage will help break the taboo surrounding her case so that similar crimes stop being unpunished.

I heard these crimes are not severely punished on other planets. Even if I want to explore the universe, I am scared to end up in a place where there's a generalized sense of impunity when it comes to women. Listen and Silent are still my favorite anagrams.

***

I'm sure everybody cares now, so I must acknowledge something. My mom would shout: "It's okay, tell them, Babygirl!"

Well, I made silly comments about Rumor Girl's "room-reading fails" back in August, and oh boy, they have me mortified today.

If my karma is taking my trash self out, I'll embrace it proudly, carrying a fancy *Makesensiaga* bag. Before I add anything, please note I'm faxing love and best wishes to the whole world, no matter what.

I usually take pride in never falling into easy traps, but The Killdeer-style camouflage on this one was top-tier. As per what I'm reading in the Tales' article covering their quarrel, it appears that Rumor Girl is allegedly not only a victim of a smudge campaign but also a victim of persecution from Giudizio.

I did not see that coming, nor did I see an actual lawsuit being filed. I feel bad; I'm incredibly regretful for Rumor Girl's suffering as she launches a trial against Giudizio.

One thing is sure, if any of them has a skeleton or black doves in their closet, it will be dug and "Nosferatued" as the dedicated special task force would say in their lingo.

Giudizio considers this a serious matter that no one should joke about. That's why he's committed to speaking up and giving his side of the story as he claps back with a counter-lawsuit.

It's happening; Giudizio is suing... *New Dork Tales Magazine* for defamation regarding what he calls "a despicable one-sided article with sprinkles of lies."

Again, I'm not a legal expert, but I would have expected him to sue Rumor Girl, not the *Tales*.

Maybe that's coming next. Unless he's guilty of something....

In any case, he's asking for compensatory damages, ξ500 xillions for reputational damages, and expected opportunity loss for his publishing company. It's my sign to keep myself to myself and leave the judgment to an Invictan legal court.

However, I'm sure the nosy tabloid fandom would love access to all their epistolary literature and recordings proving the alleged offenses by both parties. We shall see if they'll get what they want and if the outcome will be as cataclysmic as Paloma papers.

Right now, "he said she said," there are haunting smutty voice notes to uncover while Rumor Girl's husband, Breyan, and a toothless princess of dragons are also involved in the mess.

Please don't shoot the candid *messenger*; it may culminate in a lose-lose situation. If there hadn't been serious accusations behind this case, I would have just concluded that it is Logic 101, an example of too many cooks spoiling the stew.

It is a small consolation for busybodies that this real-life drama is more entertaining than their favorite tabloid. My predicting it would end with fuss makes me believe I have a gift of clairvoyance.

I keep convincing myself that the planets are aligning for me: "As we come closer to the year of the Wool Snake, my zodiac sign is poised for exhilarating career changes and a newfound happiness that will make me smile from ear to ear."

I'm up for it as long as I don't end up with a creepy Joker smile.

***

My insomnia kicks in, and I fall into a horoscope rabbit hole in the Xieta Verse until 3 am. I conclude that I'm a colossal cow cosplaying a horse fascinated by dragons and supposed to love tigers, snakes, and goats. I know I sound insane. I guess my high school teacher wasn't lying when he told the class that sleep deprivation is dangerous and could even kill.

Why am I even awake? It's a tricky time, late enough to sip cocktail drinks and early enough to start my favorite Italican coffee extraction process. I'd still like to sleep, so I quaff a Royal Smile cocktail while exploring the Xieta Verse.

Scrolling down with half-closed eyes, I come across the photo of a mysterious Invictan smiling. Seconds later, I realize the photo is spreading virally around the world. Here starts Mario's frenzy.

Who's Mario? Why are ladies and lords drooling over him?

A week ago, Mario was a complete unknown. Today, he's... Mario, a hooded person of interest with a ravishing smile. I can't believe I stayed up all night to see the break of day.

Before I fall asleep, I have a little confession: a charming smile is my second kryptonite, and a sexy smile is my Achilles heel.

"E che cazzo, Mario! Non dirmelo Mario! Cosa è successo Mario?"

I was dreaming about a simple and peaceful life in Beautiful Boot Land when I woke up to the sound of the Xieta Verse's notifications. It's blowing up, literally. Now, I need to know more about Mario, who has just been spotted and thus arrested.

I cross the street to get more information from my venerable neighbor, Dorothy. I affectionally call her Dotie, and I admit that I always try to find an excuse to check on her since her rocket scientist husband, Theodore, departed Planet X for a one-way trip to explore the Sagittarius constellation. Surrounded by vintage floral wallpapers as old as the hills, we sit by her fireplace with a cup of White Darling tea.

Then, as a good tattler, Dotie shares everything she knows or guesses about the man.

She continues her monologue while rearranging her trinkets; I listen:

"Let me break it down for you, Seely. It's all happening in Invictus Land's Tales City. This is the alleged story of a hopeless man...

Out of the blue, Mario allegedly received a mysterious invitation card in his letterbox a month ago. No name or address was indicated on the black envelope; he could only read written in pink: "Play Fair."

Inside the envelope, a sour belt candy and a minimalist invitation card dated 44.X2.XX24 depicted four geometric shapes: a triangle, a pentagon, an oval, and a cross. Mario is said to know the meaning of that invitation he had already received two years ago. It's an invitation to play the terrifying and secretive Octopus Game, in which no fore-play should be expected.

The moment he saw the slight changes in shapes, he figured it was not the same game he played. A player taking part in the game twice is never heard of, but The Adventurer (as his friends call him) is always up for a challenge. It was now or never for Mario.

Without saying anything to anyone, Mario woke up at 4 am on 44. X2.XX24, he hit the gym, then took a bike ride along Sulley River that he continued between Tales City's skyscrapers, following a sinusoidal path.

That's how Mario allegedly unintentionally ran over The Co-bra, who was crossing the street. The Cobra was rushed to a near-by high-tech hospital, where he sadly succumbed to his injury later that day. There are rumors about research and development made on cryogenics that might reverse our fates in the future. Until then, I wish to send flowers to his loved ones to show my profound and sincere sympathy. The Cobra was a loving family man and a successful entrepreneur – CEO of 4D Insurance, Invictus Land's biggest space travel insurance company.

I don't know what happened to empathy, Seely. I'm outraged and compassionate towards The Cobra's family's ordeal, but all do not share my feelings in Invictus Land.

Some shady methods used by the space travel insurance company prevent Invictans from feeling for the victim. Talers are doing what they do best, pretending they didn't see or hear anything. Some joke-sters who want to help Mario at all costs even make light of the tragedy by offering him obviously fake alibis. If you believe them all, at the time of the offense, Mario was in bed with his girlfriend, on a plane en route to Angels City with a friend, fishing with companions, partying with the whole town, and smoking with a dog sitter.

The only verified information is that four words were carved on the bike's wheels: Declare, Decline, Discharge, Dismiss. Mario explained he was a 4D Chess player and claimed his innocence. These four words have investigators suspecting that it was a quadruple threat, deducting that it wasn't an accident, but a premeditated act.

I'm still waiting for more information, and speculations continue swirling over The Adventurer's life before the terrible event.

Maybe he suffered from hallucinations after eating the sour belt candy? Supposedly, he once tried to walk on water.

Perhaps he was too worried about the upcoming Octopus Game?

Maybe it was just his fate he couldn't escape?

These questions might remain unanswered forever... But you know what, Seely? As my beloved Theodore would have said... Play unfair games, win unfair prizes."

"That's a lot to uncover, Dotie. This sad story reminds me of one of my godfather's favorite tales: the story of John B, a desperate father left with no choice other than taking desperate measures to save his son's life. But regarding this young Mario, remember Dotie, innocent till proven guilty," I reply while letting out a heavy sigh of despair before resuming to sip my tea.

When I return home, I lie down to let it all sink in.

Behind the façade of the ultra-funny girl I have displayed my whole life, I now discern every deep conversation, and every bad news is a soul eater to me. I predicted everything could happen in XX24, but it's all getting out of hand.

Before I have time to butt out of this matter, I receive another piece of information from the Xieta Verse: we shouldn't applaud the detectives for catching the alleged culprit.

"Who should we clap for?"

"The Big Monald employee who spotted him ordering a Big O burger and snitched on him."

Cooperating and tipping might be more suited to describe the snitch's actions.

Anyway, while I'm having an internal writing debate, I have another pop-up from the Xieta Verse.

No way! A movie-style perp walk!

Mario 'The Adventurer' is being extradited, and on arrival in Tales City, the entire world gets to see him being walked by, surrounded by Bad Man and heavily armed special forces.

Perfect eyebrows and prestine matching sneakers can't mute the clanking of his chains. I don't know how it will end for him, but the saddest part is Mario losing his smile.

You know what? Maybe he's innocent, and the jury will save him from a wrongful sentence.

If convicted, he may be pardoned like Folsom or end up in prison hoping to break out with the help of Zora, Shoefield, Sugar, and Thee Bag. Maybe not. Sometimes, speculations should just be left on the side. We'll know how it will dissolve sooner than later.

***

I didn't have to wait too long for another bad thing to happen.

Is Tales City cursed? When I visited last year, I thought I had found my haven. The only thing standing between me and my Tales City residency was money, considering how expensive life is there.

That was before it got clear that Talers' legendary unbothered attitude could be a problem in crucial times, like seeing a woman being set on fire in a flying metro. What happened to basic reflexes, like trying to extinguish a fire or seeking help when you encounter one? I can't even finish that newspaper article about the gruesome act. They call it the "bystanders' effect;" I call it the "doom living effect."

We live in a world where the abundance of cruelty turns people into apathetic sociopaths who would rather film people fighting for their lives than save them. Belonging to the Xieta Verse's monetized club seems more important than anything else.

It is stated in the article that a police officer also flew by, unconcerned. Well, at least I'm not surprised by that one. Thanks to Xonya Maze's distressing case in July, I know who I won't call if I need help one day.

But I refuse to lose hope; I refuse to lose my smile. We are more alike than we are different, and I'll have a crisis negotiator convince all Xians to heal the world together.

***

What seems to heal some Xians is X Must time.

X Must is a holiday partly celebrated on Planet X. Originally commemorating what some believe to be the original story of Planet X's creation, Invictus Land then rebranded it as a gift fest in which Samba Klaas has the leading role.

Samba Klaas' character comes from a millenary-old Tulips Land legend, as seen in the remains of engraved woodcuts depicting an elderly man gifting toys with a fireplace and stockings in the background. When Hope Union descendants migrated to Invictus Land, the legend became a reality boosted by consumerism, making it what it is now.

A great poet named Moore was among the first to describe what a Samba visit would look like.

Since then, parents have told their kids to write a letter to Samba explaining why they deserve all items mentioned on their wish list.

To convince them to be exemplary kids, parents narrate the story of the "right jolly old elf" with his present-loaded sleigh pulled by his flying reindeer through the stars at night.

Before going to bed, kids happily brush their teeth and prepare a glass of milk and a plate of cookies for Samba, leaving them by the chimney. Despite being depicted as a body-positive male figure, Samba is supposed to squeeze through the tight chimney bearing the requested gifts he will leave by the X Must tree.

Some try to demystify the legend, and people like me never had the occasion to believe in it. That happens when you have insensitive older siblings or clumsy parents who give you a budget and make you wrap your own gifts.

Beliefs aside, happy times!

I love this time of the year when Xians rush to light shops to decorate their houses and pine trees. I sometimes wonder how one can afford the bills that come with it, but that's not the subject.

One of my recurrent silly dreams is to go to the mountains and chop a pine tree. On my way back, of course, my car would break down in a remote area with no service or signal. No, it's not a nightmare.

Guess who would pass by me, stop his car, and tow me back to my hometown? All-Time Crush! X Must Magic...

I'd invite him to my little cottage for a Vanilla Chai tea. We would watch His Grace The Kount and Her Grace The Kountess, happy and healthy at the official carol ceremony.

We could continue our magical night with a Halie & Mark movie. Then, alternating between deep conversations and funny jokes, we'd watch Caria Maray's annual X Must hymns concert.

Guess who would attend that year? Robean and family! The street artist would enjoy the show, and she would be seen leaving all smiles with an additional Adam and Eve tattoo on her flawless skin.

Thereafter, we would get deeper into our X Must spirit while listening to the same eight songs that a hundred singers have covered.

It couldn't feel more like a dream at twilight until the perfect gentleman would tell me it's time for him to leave. I'd escort him to my door while unnecessarily rearranging my hair. He'd open the door; letting the fog and the extremely cold weather join the conversation.

He'd say: "I like your X Must wreath on the door."

A compliment to which I'd nod stupidly, not finding anything to say.

He'd get closer to me to continue with: "Old-Time Seely... Who would have thought we would ever meet again?... It was a pleasure... Good night and sweat dreams."

That's when he'd kissed my cheek in slow motion.

I'd laugh, letting go an awful snort, diminishing drastically my chances to walk down the aisle of the Chapel of Love or, should I say, to walk down the nave of a little white chapel.

He'd laugh, too. Then he'd look at me, and I'd look at him.

We'd look at each other in complete silence.

My heart would rush, and his heart would speed up. Both our rapid inhaling and exhaling would form an epic, heart-shaped glittery water vapor, merging in a beautiful Fujiwara effect.

And this is when my snooze alarm always crushes my heart.

***

The little peaceful bracket was too beautiful to be true.

While trying to stop my occasional Samba Baby ringtone, my finger hit a Xieta Verse pop-up instead. Again, it's gruesome news. Not everyone can experience a ferric, happy, and peaceful X Must holiday.

Indeed, the courageous people of Geranium Land are going through what seems more like a disaster holiday. What happened?

A desperate man committed a vile act on an X Must market there. In a twist of fate, I'm told the defeatist evildoer had dedicated his life to preventing disturbed people from committing such acts, listening to all their predicaments without judging, and finding solutions and treatments for those diagnosed with emotional, mental, or behavioral disorders.

How can one go from being optimistic to cure hopelessness to being downhearted beyond remedy? Maybe that's the aftermath of a long-term emotional dump, caring too much about things he couldn't control, or it's just the result of evil extremist beliefs.

As the offender has now departed Planet X, we might never know.

All we know is that one second, happy-go-lucky innocent people were having themselves a Merry Little X Must, and the next, it was grief wrapped up in a bow.

I wish I could find a way for the world never to have to witness one man's foolishness, causing terror and disrupting beautiful starlings' murmuration for good.

Just like we are observing a new bird flu outbreak, we are facing a desperation pandemic that has lasted too long to my taste.

Who and/or what is the culprit? Is it a medical issue, financial stress, a relationship heartbreak, loneliness, an endless pursuit of happiness, a lack of self-love, or... a lack of hope? The worst would be a combination of them all, which could be fatal.

I want to avoid that for myself and any Xian who is alive right now. Can we find a way to solve this and help each other? I don't have the solution yet, but we're all in this Blue X Must together.

We don't have a choice; it's stick season, so we must stick together.

***

While the People in Invictus Land are trying to mind their golden eggs and energy prices, The Phoenix's agenda and new map are slowly being revealed. If I understand correctly, his strategy slightly extends Invictus Land's territory. You would ask me how, maybe...

Apparently, the Great White North Land next door is appealing to him, and he wishes to make it the 14th Land of the United Lands of Invictus. His beautiful prey is the cradle of Great Northians, led by The Beaver locally and supervised by His Highness The Unicorn as it's part of Great Banter Land's *Seldom Wealth Treaty*.

Located on the northern border, it is also known as Invictus Land's Hat or Maple Syrup Land and Great Northians are not looking for a new Land Lord. Even local figure ice skaters turned counterpunchers are willing to enter the boxing ring to make their point across.

On top of this Land, another one is surprisingly on The Phoenix's new acquisitions' list: Evergreen Land, cradle of Evergreenlanders, located in Planet X's North Pole. This cold realm – the jewel of Cookie Land and essentially part of the United Viking Lands – has been ruled by His Emperor Ritzy X since his mom's abdication this year.

Cookie Land and its ally – Hope Union, both confirm Evergreen Land is "not for sale." Evergreen Land is mainly known for its penguins and genius inhabitants who overcame extreme cold and hostile environments. I'm no expert in geopolitical matters, but I would be surprised if penguins and igloos were the main reason for this sudden interest from The Phoenix.

Maybe a friend of his from the *landside* encouraged him to buy dirt, and he's following his advice. Take it from me: I bet his friend never mentioned that Great White North Land or Evergreen Land should be sought, as everybody knows they're not on the market.

For us flabbergasted folks far away from Invictus Land, we thought it was just a joke. But the next thing you know, another piece of news makes the headlines. The Phoenix now wants to take control of the Paloma Canal. Same story here; the Paloma Canal is not for sale and is owned by Paloma Land, the cradle of Palomanians. It took 400 years and thousands of lost souls to build this canal, so I doubt Palomanians will give it to anyone who knocks on their door and asks to host the party. I believe joining the party with diplomacy wouldn't be an issue, though.

Neighbors issues baffle me, and despite my nyctohylophobia, I'm getting more and more tempted to live in those remote houses only surrounded by woods.

If I can even find a remote area with no broadband connection – not even Exron's Rocket Science technology called Moonlink, I might finally be able to meditate, be happy, and reach my goal. From Dack Jersey to Steave Works, I don't know if it's a myth that meditation is key for some of these zillionaires, but I might need to cure my self-diagnosed ADHD first if I want to stop thinking about my next meal or what would happen if I don't clock in at work the next day. Like pollution, there's always a new worry soiling my mind, and I'm pretty sure I'm not the only Xian who experiences this.

***

Speaking of zillionaires, maybe inspired by The Phoenix, Exron is allegedly working on enhancing his body with mechanical wings. While his secret lab is allegedly working on that project, he's fighting with Walky-Pedia, the walking know-it-all robot built by the people and available for free for every Xian.

What's his issue with the robot everyone has and never complained about (except for a few accuracy adjustments)?

The robot is allegedly becoming too polite, non-allergic to equity, and acknowledging minorities instead of insulting them as he would have programmed. Exron is allegedly urging geniuses at the origin of the robot's creation to stop funding its maintenance.

Luckily, I still have *my* Walky-Pedia at home, and it's still walking. Let's hope my Walky-Pedia never quits or stops working because of an external party's action. I would get it if the robot resigned due to its defect, though, as The Gator did.

The Gator is one of The Phoenix's allies. Originally only known for his love for animals, he has been picked and propelled by The Phoenix to become the Lord of Justice in Invictus Land.

This is when the cobbler's children go barefoot, as it appears The Gator is being investigated for several crimes. Isn't it ironic? I doubt he thinks so, as he has to give up his short-lived increased power.

***

As already explained, most of the lessons I've learned come more from comprehending people's mistakes than from understanding my boring and insignificant experiences. The same patterns keep repeating like waves in the ocean. Stupid decisions and actions made when one feels invincible prevent them from making their dreams come true. Yes, everybody makes mistakes.

Let's be clear: I'm far from perfect, but I'm among the luckiest Xians born to be good, so I don't have to fight too much against my nature. I naturally try to be irreproachable and will always try to avoid any crime, destructive behavior, unnecessary fights, or hate speech. Because I know that hate is a dangerous game.

I do not like receiving or giving unsolicited advice, but if you read this and reckon it's not natural for you to avoid easy traps, think about it as making sure nothing comes between you and your biggest dream if the opportunity comes to fulfill it one day.

I personally only need to be able to look myself in the mirror; some don't care and count on privilege, money, and power games to achieve their wildest dreams, whether or not they deserve it.

***

Everyone should always be ready to suffer the consequences of their mistakes. Remember Tim Lake, whose swimming show was almost ruined in June because of his mishap? Scrutiny of his every move continues, and word on the beach is that his swim brief nearly got torn during the Invictan Men Freestyle race.

No stranger to wardrobe malfunctions by association, he handled it better than that time when Janice (his teammate on the Mixed 4x100 Relay race) endured humiliation from a defective swim trunk 20 years ago. Not many people supported the innocent woman back then, but voices are rising right now to demand "justice for Janice."

Maybe it was the same people who freed Brie Brie, her dance moves, and her knives. The world (and evidently Tim Lake) also failed to support Brie Brie, who was unjustifiably controlled and betrayed. The only things left to free are her nose block and air fryer. A part of me still wishes I could be as free-spirited as Brie Brie. Another part of me is just like her; I am not a girl anymore, but I am not sure I can be a woman yet. I somehow refuse to grow up unless life makes me.

Anyway, I was talking about Janice. Who is she? She's part of a five-child family called the Invictan G5, which is known for its greatness in the sports industry. Janice's fans want to protect her at all costs. Even more so, her invincible brother, The King, has left Planet X too soon to heal the Solar System and make the Milky Way a better galaxy. Additionally, when I went to cheer Janice up during her swimming race in Big Smoke City in September, I heard that her other brother, The Honorable, also recently departed Planet X to go where his heart is, to the place where magic happens, the one-way interplanetary superhighway.

One thing is sure: I'll never get used to people leaving.

Even if it's strangers, it's always heart-wrenching to say goodbye.

***

After his farewell to the NSL world at the beginning of the year, we finally know what the future holds for Ball Chicbelly. No, the best NSL coach in Invictan history will not start a new journey in the professional polo league; he will continue to coach stud poker – but at university in Tar Heel City, the cradle of Tar Heelers, located in the Invictan North. We can only congratulate him and wish him well for his youthful journey ahead, which was his long-forgotten dream.

I, too, want to get to the other side of my seven-year project, but all this non-stop noise this month always makes me forget I'm supposed to chase my dream. At least it's a friendly reminder that it's never too late, and I shouldn't give up.

Rosh Hulen would agree! Who? Rosh Hulen! For the first time, the man received the accolade he's always dreamed of: NSL's Most Voracious Player (MVP). Rosh Hulen is a part-time blueberry farmer, but still among the greatest stud poker players in Invictus Land this year. So many highlights justify his win; his great team players also helped him get the precious prize.

I'm still running out of time, so I can't get into more details, but some critics say Malar Batson should have won MVP instead, as Hulen's professional status is still unclear due to his commendable farming duties. Malar Batson is also one of the greatest and he even broke historical poker records this year.

You might wonder why Mr. Record Man didn't win MVP... I am, too, and the shortest explanation I got is: "Rosh Hulen has more valuable moments that were detrimental to his team's winning, and Malar Batson had a spectacular record-breaking year individually that didn't transpose to his team winning more." Maybe Malar Batson should clone himself to ensure he gets his third MVP.

In any manner, I'm happy for Rosh Hulen, who deserves that award and 52 more!

I know someone else from the NSL world who deserves happiness, love, and support, too. Who? The illustrious and freaky Franky Muss! The legendary man known to be one of the fastest NSL players just announced he is going through difficult times but is thriving and surviving. Keep your head up, Prince! We need you. I never have the right words, but my compassion is sincere.

Sometimes, I wish I could have better oratory skills. My father or my godfather, Uncle Wenz, would have the perfect words for the situation. My dad would say, "Word of mine, it's going to be alright," and Uncle Wenz would say, "Burdensome circumstances shouldn't dictate your happiness and your inner peace as long as you have faith."

If someone deserves that Medal of Freedom, it's Uncle Wenz.

***

I want to reach the same level of wisdom independently of arduous times. I'm always doing pretty good until I get stuck in disbelief when the unthinkable occurs.

The last example I have in mind is how impotent I feel about tragic stories of fallen supersonic butterflies. Supersonic butterflies are new high-tech vessels transporting Xians around our vast planet and beyond. Along with supersonic planes, flying them is Planet X's safest means of transportation, considering stringent regulations and procedures to ensure a minimum risk of error or accident.

It had been a while since a Supersonic Butterfly had made the headlines until the end of December XX24. The first major accident of the year happened in the Eternal Fire Land, the cradle of the Eterni people, located in the big Region I (+; +) surrounding Golden Eagle Land. Investigations are ongoing, but the Supersonic Butterfly is alleged to have been struck by a foreign object. A meteorite or another stellar object might be responsible. I only know that there were innocent Xians with fallen dreams who were sadly affected.

A few days later, the dark series of accidents continues in Red Dragon Land with another Supersonic Butterfly that meets a flock of birds and ends in tragedy. Natural birds still fail to recognize Supersonic Butterflies as different as them and keep trying to make contact, causing disastrous and regrettable events. I wish Engineering tycoons could reunite to find a solution to this problem. It boggles my mind that we can reach all our faraway Moons, but we cannot send signals repelling little birds to avoid catastrophes. Again, I'm at a loss for words able to give some relief and moral support to families impacted.

Maybe I can try to write a poem on the spot.

***

Goodbye, Butterfly

A fallen Supersonic Butterfly
Smiling souls reaching the sky
To decorate the Stars with their art
Leaving a millstone on crying hearts

Departing for good but staying forever
In our memory always, despite our bond severed
Lucky us with delayed and missed trains
Until we spread our wings to meet lost angels again

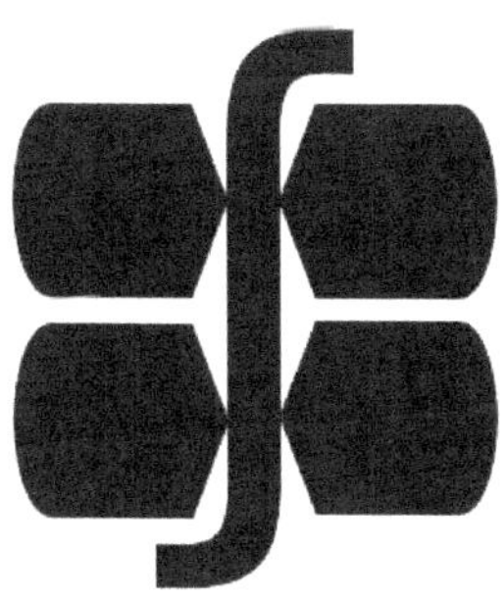

How are we getting out of this? Is there anything positive this month at all? Like my little old-soul nephew Chad once told his teacher at school: "Well, let me tell you something, Ms Miranda. I need a break from everything and everyone. I want to check out and enjoy the rest of my life" – and I couldn't relate more.

That's when entertainment matters – to escape from our tortured lives. Let's return to the dedicated, happy blog on the Xieta Verse.

Finally, some great news! Mrs. Invictana is closing her *Auras* tour in style after 3-2-1 years and sharing her hard-earned money with the whole planet!

My best colleague would say: "Girl needs to rest, for real."

They say, "Listen to your body." Well, her body doesn't seem ready to retire at all! Maybe hyperactivity keeps her in her salad days. The young-spirited woman is aging like fine wine, and while hinting at new beginnings for her next theatre adventures, rumors of her character assassination are surfacing, too.

Remember the Rumor Girl chronicles scandal? Apparently, Giudizio is alleging that Mrs. Invictana is not a Xian but a four-winged dragon in disguise. It has become a legal matter dealt with by public opinion. When it will involve a proper court, let's hope no vaping witness will tell us a dragon stepped on a bee, no attorney will object on their own question, and no pint of wine will be needed for this one.

Luckily, Mrs. Invictana does not let haters get under her skin, which she doesn't grudge to shed to keep it as glossy as a snake's. From the vigilante little black dress with the girl squad to a tea-style Gingham armor with Wild Valentine, she's consistently winning.

Whether Smarties or whoever like it, Wild Valentine is a keeper. No more pearl-clutching or unfounded worries from anyone; he's Mr. Perfectly OK now. No love scam with this one! How do I know? The

NSL star put together an elaborate and splendid *Auras*-coded party to celebrate the end of *The Auras*! So creative and cute!

The recent clouded skies almost made me forget about this couple's best invention: LOVE! If they can spread it around with all their fellow lovers, I won't protest! Planet X needs it, desperately!

***

My internal dialogue is at it again:

"Yee Haw! She's back!"

"Who?"

"You know who!"

"The one and only Queen V!"

She's wearing all white everything – unfiltered, undisturbed, un-tethered. That's the spirit of X Must!

She's releasing a surprise movie she's directing and starring in.

Stupid me, who only picked the brains – Queen V is proof that you can choose beauty AND brains. The new movie is a masterpiece for which she might get an O'Star or a Granite award. It's a revolutionary mix celebrating Mother Land's history, Invictan pre-eminence, cultural progress, and greatness.

While watching the movie, I laugh uncontrollably about an inside joke I have to say out loud: "All this time, she was Betty with the good hair!" (*chuckles*)

Queen V always fought to fix the Invictan cultural divide and is so generous and inclusive that she brought a lot of new up-and-coming actors like Cowboy Boo and her big town's Postman.

Postman went from hood parody to sending burnt cover letters to Mrs. Invictana to apply for her space trip, and now he's living the simple life while starring in a blockbuster with Queen V.

No one can look at Postman's decorated face and tell him he's not living a high-powered dream.

Guess who's also making a surprise cameo in the movie?

Her daughter, the adorable Yellow! She's got her parents' genes!

She's such a natural entertainer whose future can only be bright!

I also heard the mother-daughter duo did a documentary together: *Animal Kingdom in Mother Land*. It must be amazing to share these baby steps in the entertainment industry with your Superstar mom and your Jeydi dad right by your side. In the same way, it must be so special to see your blood heritage gradually taking over.

The only fly in the ointment is that many accusations have been made about The Jeydi since the debacle with The Dandy. Rumors are getting serious, and people are wondering if he should be side-eyed. I never join the public opinion court. Let's wait and see if it's going to end with a lawsuit withdrawal. But as usual, when the rumor mill starts, scrutiny follows, and new conspiracy theories emerge daily. There are even despicable people who are criticizing Yellow's fashion sense now. Luckily, the B-list defense counterattacks, explaining that "she's a toddler, and if there is any faux pas, her personal shopper should be criticized, not her." * Bang! * End of the debate.

Like Queen V, if you're closing the door on useless drama, you may as well do it with a bang!

Fast forward a few weeks: Queen V is announcing the shooting of a sequel to her Western movie called *The Cheater Links.*

Word on Dave's *Lucky Stuff*'s beehive is that she will do auditions and filming in several Invictan cities, Frawn Land's Love City, and GB Land's Big Smoke City.

The inclusive woman is even inviting amateurs to apply if they believe they have talent. We never know, I could get out of my Camelia Street's den to audition as an extra. No matter what, this is my time to shine.

If I don't get the part, at least I'll be able to visit the big town and pass by my favorite FragranCe store to buy my *Adored* perfume by Charisse x Robean.

I'm willing to pay to watch the shooting, though. As I'm sparing my remaining kidney and my liver's value is uncertain, I don't know what vital organ I will sell to be in the queue. Let's hope the infamous ticket vending machine that usually takes care of live audience seats will fix their nerve-wracking technical issues by then and won't seize the opportunity to extort applicants.

***

When I watch Queen V elegantly riding her sublime horse, line dancing in between shotgun scenes, and perfectly giving a nod to rodeo culture in Invictus' Western movies, I recall my first horseback riding lessons in high school. I've always been fascinated by horses and their silent healing power, but the majestic animal is more impressive in real life than on TV.

On my first day at Requiem Equestrian Center, preppy-styled me had her riding boots on and her helmet tightly locked, but was acutely scared to enter the stable. From afar, I could hear a bluegrass tune being played. As a young girl from a small town in Great Banter Land, that was my first introduction to Invictan music.

You might find it silly, but it felt like home, as if I knew it from a past life, and I started walking more confidently towards my dedicated, beautiful Paint Horse, Cobalt. I don't know how it happened, but no words, no touch, just a look, and I felt trust at first sight with Cobalt.

Then Beckett, my equine coach that I hadn't met yet, barged into the stable and urged me to tack up Cobalt. Rumor has it that the young Invictan man had left his cherished *landside* to follow his Grit lover, Miranda.

It's great to know that normal people can also invent love!

Anyway, I told Beckett I didn't know what to do.

"Well, put the saddle on, get the bridle in, get your feet on the stirrups, and ride that shit," he said with a strong Invictan *landside* accent.

"I beg your pardon?" I shyly asked

"You look rode hard and put up wet. You won't hear me tell *ya* to bless your heart, Seely. Toughen up, butter cup! In ten minutes, you'll either be riding that horse, or you won't be allowed back in here," he added while giving me the boot.

Sometimes, an ultimatum works, and Beckett's twang is doing its tang. With what I discovered later to be Roots and Invictana music on the backdrop, I saddled Cobalt and was riding it in 10 minutes.

Yee Haw!

Cobalt is the only being on Planet X that fully understood me. Beckett and Cobalt have always been supportive and patient, not me. I struggled to transition from the bridle to the neck rope for my show jumping competitions, but Cobalt is the epitome of a ride-or-die –

always covering up my mistakes. But as always, I lacked perseverance or found another short-lived hobby, so I gave up after a few years.

Because of financial issues, Requiem Equestrian Center closed, so I have no idea where Beckett is or if Cobalt is still alive after 22 years. Yes, I asked Goodle – everyone's favorite browser, but to no avail. I'd still like to get back on track one day, though, and oh, I wish I could get back to these happier times!

Beckett would say: "If wishes were horses, beggars would ride."

***

It's my sign to stop wishing and start acting.

If I try to compute the countless hours spent on the Xieta Verse, I know I won't believe the extent of the precious time lost.

I won't lie; I enjoy every second of it, falling on rabbit holes and easy traps, perusing the lives of people I will never meet, hurting for some, praying for others but forgetting myself and my dreams in the mix. Dreaming to escape differs from dreaming to achieve. I need to start intentionally dreaming and manifesting my future. But can a dream be yours if it never appeared to you? Can you create one? Should you?

We are approaching the year's end, and I still have so many unfulfilled promises I want to correct before it's too late. But even plugged off from the Xieta Verse, I feel like the woman who can't be moved, stuck, frozen. I always find a back road to get unstuck, but this time, the dark cloud of an impending revolution seems stronger than the universe. Across Planet X, the future doesn't look too good for some people who fear they reached the sixth dimension. I, for now, refuse to lose hope there's a brighter light on the other side of December, and I won't capitulate to what my parents call irrational fears.

My beautiful worries are fueled by the Xieta Verse or people who can't respect my decision to disconnect from it.

I love my endearing neighbor Dotie. She's a good egg, but this morning, she brought inopportune news, X Must cookies, and her lemon jelly, which I never dared to confess I disliked.

She told me that The Harrier – the former Invictus Land leader who celebrated his 100 years on Planet X two months ago – slung his hook and left for good to explore the Softball Polaris Galaxy.

Dotie believes he may have exited right in time because he didn't want to take the chance to see how Invictus Land would end. At least unity is shown to pay a well-deserved tribute to The Harrier, who's remembered by all as a decent and honest man.

Note to self: act the way you want to be remembered.

Everybody showed up to the celestial take-off: The Bear, The Heron, The Phoenix, The Dolphin, and The Owl, among others.

The atmosphere is astonishingly peaceful, just like it was for my grandmother, who wanted us only to remember good memories and benevolent acts and celebrate her departure after her valiant diamond years spent with my grandfather on Planet X.

At least it confirms that when it matters, Xians can forget about their deep-seated grievances and be united.

Maybe we will all be surprised, and the world will salute their respective leaders' efforts to improve their everyday lives.

In the meantime, here I am... still listening.

13

Dreizember

HERE WE ARE... WRITING.

As days shorten in Dreizember, it's time for traditions, reflections, and transition.

When a new year starts, I usually want time to slow down because I am eager to start new ventures and see where the universe will take me. Then time passes, and it becomes clear I won't put my life or the world to rights, so I give in and want to speed it up.

Note to self: even small changes take time.

This coping mechanism is just one of many self-sabotage tricks I crave for. Another one I mastered in the past four years is stress eating, successfully supersizing me while the world is super-shrinking. But without noticing it right away, since I started my dream hunt, I am slowly detaching from my old habit of swimming against the current. I don't even remember the last time I tried to find a better scenery.

Something weird is happening; for the first time, I don't yearn to travel and escape reality.

I've stayed in my small hometown to try and digest it all.

As a member of *The Unfortunate Bunch* club, I'm just grateful for having a roof above my head, enough money to eat, and *(fingers crossed)* a relatively good health.

***

It's challenging to escape reality when the news worsens every day.

Everything feels surreal, but it's our new normal. That said, my routine is someone else's oddness, and vice versa – but different rules and experiences can make different people reach the same level of happiness.

After my Mary-style social media break, I'm logging back on the Xieta Verse and realize it's more important than ever to stay alert as distressing events from Invictus Land's Big Easy City show the devastating consequences of despair again.

Reminiscent of events in Geranium Land last month, dirty angels driving runaway cars are again committing irreparable and unforgivable cowardly acts.

Big Easy City is located in the south of Invictus Land. It is known for its delicious food, rhythm & blues, party spirit, inclusivity, and mostly its colorful and welcoming inhabitants. So, it's tough to recover from the contrast between the jovial city and the atrocity of such a crime.

Again, we are witnessing the derailing of innocent people's destinies. I can only regret the madman didn't miss the execution of his vile plan like the one who failed in his attempt at hurting one of Xians' venerated men, Papa Fratello.

I will never understand these actions – never.

If one wants to explore the stars before their calling occurs, no one should be forced to join them, especially not kids.

I can't help but think about young Xians who feel resigned to succumbing to frightful acts in a seemingly senseless world.

The most devastating are the tricky cases of young Invictan forcing fellow youngsters to join them on their doomed Yolo's astral arches. I try to respect Invictan *Second Act* and ball-trap traditions, but this hobby seems incompatible with a desperation pandemic.

That epidemic is spreading to every layer of Invictan society without discrimination, and no one seems safe. Whether it's a teenage boy from Volunteer City blinded by self-hate or a lonely outcast teenage girl from Badger City who chooses forced departures, I know it can't be the only solution.

That's why I think it's important that everyone starts the smile hunt for themselves and the greater good. By doing so, chances are that what seems essential and heavy will become insignificant.

Remember what we've been told before a supersonic plane take-off: "In case of depressurization, put your oxygen mask on first." If you don't, you might end up suffocating before the person you're trying to save or, more generally speaking, feel obliged to finish someone else's fight that doesn't really concern you.

While actual malefactors hide and thrive, people jump into unsuitable situations that may ruin their lives. It would be unfortunate to do so without trying to reconnect with their inner child's dreams.

The goal here is having fun, finding something that can genuinely make oneself smile on a bad day without thinking about fame or capital gain – no overthinking; a great surface-level pleasure.

For people who have already had the chance to explore it, please share it with whoever is interested and encourage others to follow their path.

Please make sure not to have any expectations of people's reactions, as we all know that Xians are complex beings who might not always show love when it's deserved. On days when it'll be more difficult to cope, let's all try to take a deep breath, disconnect from the Xieta Verse if it feels too heavy, connect with people on our simple distractions, and seek help whenever we feel like it.

***

While I'm literally pulling my hair with my forlorn hope of healing Planet X's desperation pandemic, I have a presentiment that another kind of epidemic is starting to spread simultaneously.

As I've been trying to wean myself off the Xieta Verse, I've missed a lot of things.

First, The Phoenix has something to celebrate – he's *Tales'* Person of the Year XX24.

This is his world now, and we're living in it.

The Phoenix is known for his gravitas but his supporters swear "he is also fun and energetic." MISA partisans are all chanting in the streets, "Finally, some action! The snoring fest is over."

If I understand correctly, it's also time for the official leader baton pass between The Turtle and The Phoenix in Invictus Land, and some untoward gestures are made. The "who's who" of "own what?" is at The Phoenix's inauguration party, and everybody bows to them. Looking at the aggregated net worth of the first row, some compare it to a dark romance between money and power and believe that the capital bubble took control of Invictus Land – for better or worse.

An Invictan King is born, and during his acceptance speech, The Phoenix expresses his gratitude to Exron, who "knows the rules of *SYTYCR* and computer games better than anyone" and asks the public to give him a standing ovation. NO COMMENT.

At this exact moment, Exron, who gave the impression of being just an extra in *The CEOs* movie, takes a lead role. Deja-vu feeling, Exron stiffly joins the stage with his signature off-beat clapping.

There is no judgment here, especially as Exron is allegedly self-diagnosed with AuDHD; I'm just describing things as they are, as my imaginary therapist asked me to do.

Here begins a shift when Exron's alleged disorder pretendedly gains control of his body right when he shows his love to the crowd and admiration for The Phoenix. The gesture, evocative of dark times well explained to me in depth during my visit to Chocolate City's ILHM Museum in November, is apparently wrongly interpreted by sensitive people. Exron and his supporters are allegedly urging everybody to check their eyesight, as he's stating that it was "evidently just a heartfelt and awkward display of joy" similar to his jumping on the toasting stage a few months ago. Well, the jumping is here to stay, just like his "clumsy" and "regrettable" enthusiastic gestures – to put it lightly.

In good faith and allegedly to avoid a smudge campaign and convince the world they should continue to inflate his bank account, zillionaire Exron embarked on a PR-orchestrated historical visit to Geranium Land. NO COMMENT.

To all intents and purposes, the treacherous overtone of Exron's newfound manners at a public and official event is minacious to Invictan peace. It might even contaminate the world in a domino effect.

Before the ink is dry, my worst nightmare is becoming a reality. Distasteful incidents are arising in Invictus Land and rapidly pollute fragile minds worldwide. While Invictans seem paralyzed by the atrocious times they are witnessing, Hope Union is marching for their freedom and peace. I'm still agoraphobic, so even if December is over, I won't judge anyone who chooses not to protest, either.

Anyway, I just have an eerie feeling that history repeats itself.

For the first time, I want to be wrong so badly.

****

Astronomers discerned that most objects of the Kuiper Belt adhere to orbits that cluster together unless there's an astral object that can apply an opposite force that will pull them away from each other. Maybe the same postulate can explain what draws all the Power Bros together.

Who are they? No need to introduce you to The Phoenix and all his influential friends, among which Xieta Verse's founders (Exron, Zu Berger, El Jefe), Sunny Pitch, Sim Hutman, Gersey Brim, Robert Morph, Tom Cool, and Gerard Bernaud.

Their mantra: "Bros over pros, Bros over Rose."

People used to think there was some rivalry between them, but not at all, and their newfound bromance is just mesmerizing to see.

Okay, let's not exaggerate. Since Exron is targeting Sim Hutman's business, the duo seems at odds about who should accept a hostile takeover bid. Sim Hutman allegedly empathizes with Exron's insecurities and wishes his peer's happiness.

With a newly gained self-confidence, Zu Burger doesn't have time for silly quarrels. Among all Power Bros' glow-ups, his dramatic change is the most visible with his new sense of fashion as he's now sporting golden chains and diamond grillz while attending the weekly frat house parties in The Phoenix's lavish South Lagoon property. Power Bros can count on him to bring swimming towels.

***

Evidence also shows no astral object between the Phoenix and Exron, but there might be one between The Phoenix and his beloved wife, The Osprey.

Sorry – my mistake; it was just an haute couture statement from the beautiful fashionista at her husband's inauguration party that I've mistaken for a slight. The Osprey is doing what I've been trying to do since I was born, minding her own business. While slowly introducing their alluring youngest heir named The Bison, she lets her other half and his best friend Exron rule the most powerful Land on Planet X without meddling in their affairs.

The Phoenix and Exron love each other's aphantasic brains and shout it at the top of their lungs!

You see, even when you don't think you have anything in common with someone fundamentally different, it's still possible to find common interests. I share their intense attraction to higher IQs, or more precisely, high-ranking emotional intelligence.

As an afterthought, we might not have the same definition of intellect and brainpower. Speaking of, right now, I'm losing one neocortical neuron per second. I'm reaching critical levels of brain fog.

But whether the world or Invictan People like it or not, the bestie duo is here to stay, and they must get used to that "hyper normalization" for the next five years – at least.

***

The Phoenix fully trusts his best friend, who was tasked to limit the Invictan sports industry's spending budget. Supported by seventeen chosen prodigious youngsters, Exron launches The Dodgeball Cut taskforce, also known as Exron & Sons. Created initially to audit Invictan dodgeball teams' accounts, it has now become an omnipotent entity working "in the best interests of Invictans."

Like a rat up a drainpipe, they're allegedly wiping charities, libraries, and everything considered wasteful for Invictus Land or not suiting their agenda. It's so BX13 coded.

I'm neither allergic to change nor fun, and I guess a good revolution should always look like anarchy.

In no time, Invictans may witness the Lord of Justice regaining his sight and dropping his scale – miracles are happening, and triggering exiles are expected.

For demanding nosepickers, it might look like there's no balance or respect for established institutions. However, with a refreshing ruling transparency, Exron & Sons shush their haters, and are determined to make them change sides and prove they couldn't be more wrong. Invictus Land may be entering its most progressive era.

Exron's only downside is the resignation of one of his taskforce's young geniuses, who's compelled to back out because of hatred souvenirs resurfacing from the Xieta Verse.

For those who haven't inscribed it on a Post-heat yet, I'll repeat my note to self: make sure that nothing comes between you and your most prominent dream if you get the chance to fulfill it one day.

Hate is a dangerous game that can easily culminate in a self-inflicted wound, or, as youngsters would say, FAFO.

The Power Bros and The Owl *(eyes and mouth wide opened)* are calling for the public's pardon for the boy's not-so-old and not-so-light mistake. They may have been inspired by The Phoenix's recent pardoning of the Sixth Pack Stormers, the dodgeball team demoted because of a few inconsistencies in their financial accounts from the XX21 audit – among other charges.

I guess The Turtle can't criticize that decision now.

While all this transpires, poor Exron is giving his all to his mission, and he sacrifices his luxury manor to sleep on the floor of dodgeball courts. On the other side of the world, protests continue with one slogan: "Save Exron, save his utopian martial world!"

Even if he doesn't seem to be affected by the backlash, a crumb of consolation for Exron is the unconditional support he receives from The Phoenix and the Power Bros. While he's starting to "Make Invictus Strait Again," I'm so glad he allows us to share this beautiful planet with him.

"Wait, is it Exron's world? It starts to look a lot like it."

"Silly me, it can only be The Phoenix's."

Pardon my digression, but did Exron disclose the name of the guinea pig who volunteered for his brain mic implant? Was it himself?

***

While Exron & Sons are unofficially getting VIP tent access to Invictan internal affairs, The Phoenix is tackling the scourge of costly Taenite straws and Schersite Xi pennies. Be reassured that a hypothetical stagflation shouldn't impact corporate sharks or financial wolves.

On top of that, The Phoenix is resolved to share his cartophile ideas that he has compiled in his new Planet X geography book (The Phoenix's version). We all know Planet X desperately needs a map projection amendment to represent accurate Land sizes better, but The Phoenix wasn't on my bingo card to offer that. We had some clues about his new protectionism map, but at least now it's crystal clear.

As plain as the nose on perplexed faces, Invictus Land is depicted at the center of the universe. The map legend gives more context – it is a nod to Invictus Land's mystery brick circle in Sooner City, where one can shout in the intergalactic void without being heard on Planet X.

My faulty brain doesn't allow me to concentrate enough to finish his book – but the prologue gives me an idea of how it ends. Great White North Land and Evergreen Land are nowhere to be found; Invictus Land has engulfed both. Maybe his idea of imposing new tariffs on Great White North Land, Red Dragon Land, and Paloma Land, among others, is not aimed at starting a trade war but at reshaping his beautiful territory. We'll eventually know if it's all part of a mammoth bluff. Funny enough – sorry, not sorry for being easily amused.

The Phoenix wants to spice it up with an unwanted bid on Maze Strip, Holy Land's hidden gem. Currently at war, Maze Strip is more known for its fallen angels than its white sand beaches. But I'm not a visionary, The Phoenix is, and he's determined to make Maze Strip the next Invictan tourist attraction. He can't do no wrong; he's the best!

Understanding it would mean to force all Mazestrinians out of their cherished Land and roots, most of Planet X's leaders are incapable of saluting his ingenuity and conjointly voice their disagreement with this seaside resort project.

Strangely enough, The Phoenix doesn't seem interested in the paradisiac beaches next door in Nueva Luna Land.

On the contrary, he only wants to clarify in bold red font that the Gulf of Luna is rebranded as the Gulf of Invictus.

Moreover, all Lunacans that had emigrated to Invictus Land are being encouraged to take an ICE Cream and leave, along with other unpopular foreigners. Of course, the only one not being offered an ICE Cream to return to Rainbow Land (+; –) is Exron.

It's crazy how all this reminds me of my parents warning me never to accept free candies or ICE Cream from Mr. Snacks. When I was a child, while all the kids were rushing towards the merry melody from the white ICE Cream Truck's speakers, I would triple-lock the front door.

Maybe 'That Girl' Mary has PTSD from not being able to enjoy ICE Cream when she was young, too, because the Xian rights activist is pouring her heart out on the Xieta Verse. On the face of it, the woman endowed with a scarce beauty is terrified that her family and friends could fall into the easy trap.

If I can relate to her distress, cold-hearted Invictans are mocking her, and Invictan officials are backing them up with alleged threats – tricky times, tricky times. Xian's specie is not a monolith, though, so there's not one way to react to the same problematic situation. To each their own.

I want to take the opportunity to congratulate 'That Girl' Mary on her engagement with Punny Planto. No, I hadn't forgotten them. Yes, they invented love, too. I try not to pick through people's windows and bull's eyes.

One who didn't invent love and never will is 'That Girl' Mary's coworker, Carl Moron, who's facing delayed repercussions from hatred reminders reappearing from the Xieta Verse. I have the most difficulty taking The Deer's High Road in cases like this one. I can't find the right words to express how stupid it is for someone confronted with untranslatability stalemates to be narrow-minded.

Gabe Churchelle would have the perfect punchline for that one – like, "Invictus Land sending xillions of rubbers worldwide might be a good idea after all... It could have prevented that pestilent man from having anything to say to begin with... Another rubber to Rainbow Land and Planet X may have never existed... A Frawnch letter to Great Banter Land, and we would've never had to read this garbage."

***

The world is more divided than ever.

My godfather would tell me that some people were born with the gift of annihilation – first-grade bank accounts but low-grade spirits.

Nevertheless, no one wants Invictus Land to fall down – not Uncle Squad, Jamie Socks, Shiny Tatoo, Gemar Baker, or Mortal Friedman. Everybody wants The Phoenix to fulfill his *Noble*-worthy peace-maker dream. Well, at least I do. I don't know what Invictans think anymore.

We're way past the Listening Month, and everybody is still silent as grave. The Dolphin's absence might be a necessary recovery time from having a handshake refusal from her successor's affiliate.

OK, what about the rest who were very vocal a few months prior? All tongues have been stolen! They were quick to give voting directives to their fellow Invictans, but now, we don't hear a peep.

Maybe they expect a hermit from another planet to speak up, or perhaps they're too busy organizing their privileged exodus. With her xillionaires and zillionaires friends, Dame O'Purple is allegedly packing her bags and flying away to more peaceful Lands like Italic Land or even further, on another planet. Are they leaving the Poor behind?

You know what? I might not be the best Invictan Jadeite Card candidate, but I'd go to Invictus Land to back them up if possible.

I still think it's one of the most beautiful Lands where all dreams can come true, and I still trust The Phoenix to rail it back in and make the world a better *safe*.

Call me insane or a sycophant, but in a certain way, I love everyone. I may be too naive because some ill-famed people can grow on me.

I'm not ready to give up trying and see the good in people.

***

I know The Owl would agree with me. I was scared that he had suffered a Ceres-like retrograde – but no, he's not a plant, and he's said to be the new cowboy in Delulu Town.

If anyone had forgotten, he reminds everyone that Los Rojos are still looking for "the enemy within." He found the culprit in seconds; it's Red Dragon Land!

We were waiting for that statement from Great Banter Land, which just expelled an alleged Dragonese spy, but Grits would consider it an isolated incident instead.

Inspired by Exron's recent visit to Geranium Land, The Owl destroys the "moral superiority" of Hope Union to whomever he meets there in between beers and Sauerkraut dishes. Indeed, he's allegedly tired of "meaningless sanctions" against Triple-Headed Golden Eagle Land and hinting at a pact soon-to-be signed between The Phoenix and The Libra. Remember how Hope Union – supported by The Turtle – isolated the latter? Even The Libra's close neighbors cut their electrical bonds to spread their independent energetical wings. It's in the past – now The Phoenix is back, and he's ready to change the scenario, replacing The Killdeer's unconvincing performance with The Libra's unquestionable greatness.

Along with The Owl, The Phoenix also urges everybody to use free speech! As my friend Becky would say, "Mention it all, Seely!"

It goes straight to my doubtful heart and motivates me to fulfill my resolution to be more vocal this year.

The powerful duo may never get to read this, but now I'm sure they would support me and tell Planet X how great I am!

***

Too bad, Invictus Land has more pressing matters: Angels City's paradise is burning in flames, and a southern hell is freezing over. Anything can happen, and all gates can open.

I wonder why this year started like a fairytale and ended like a jigsaw nightmare. Well, all warning signs should be written between the lines.

Maybe the dark series of birds falling from the sky in Invictus Land is the prophetic sign of Planet X's End Times.

My mental health is declining, and I think my traveling break was never a good idea. I should be somewhere catching some rays, but I'm lying in bed, obsessed with Xieta Verse news.

A little confession: I'm now scared to travel, even more so as further Supersonic Butterflies incidents occured.

First, in Brotherly Love City, the attempt to save a precious life sadly failed due to what may be a technical issue.

Second, in Chocolate City, a disastrous collision precipitated farewells due to either an intentional mistake, a miscommunication, and/or a staff shortage. Red boxes from the Supersonic Butterflies might help to find the cause and assign responsibilities.

Third, in Last Frontier City, a Supersonic Butterfly vanished to be found later severely damaged, and another single-seat one forced its pilot to evacuate.

Fourth, in Emerald City, an attempt at the ancient dab salute had two Supersonic Butterflies clip tails in the taxiway.

Fifth, in Grand Canyon City, a Supersonic Butterfly kissed another parked on a landing lane, and both ended up intertwined.

Sixth, a Supersonic Butterfly wanted to see both sides of a story and rolled over for miraculous belly rubs.

Seventh, in Optics Valley City, a midair encounter ended two Supersonic Butterflies' courting rituals.

The law of series may have just been proved. And this is without counting daily near-misses and mishaps.

The root of these terrible incidents is yet to be uncovered, and it's not only taking place in Invictus Land. I don't have enough time to learn everything about incidents in Sampa City and Frawnch's Dom Island.

One would understand why I canceled my booked trip to explore Region IV's breathtaking sceneries for the New Year. Not to sound silly, but I want to make it to XX25 alive and I'll try my best to achieve that. I'm not sure I'll indubitably skip my final destination by staying home, though.

***

Before disconnecting from the Xieta Verse to meditate for the New Year, I plug into the entertainment news digest. All these recent un-propitious events made me forget that the Granites have been delayed because of the ravaging fires in Angels City. But nothing can stop Deluwood from being tone-deaf to the parlous state of Invictus Land and Planet X – the show must go on!

The Vulture and his naked muse are trying new hate stunts again, and he's working overtime to boost his shock value. Should anyone tell him that an awkward handshake is coming his way? Irrelevant to me, scandalous for some, genius for his wannabe bestie Exron. Again, impertinent to me.

Back to the Granites where the "who's who" of "win what?" is acting as if nothing was happening in the world. Maybe I'm the crazy one...

***

I'm happy for Queen V, who's receiving her long overdue accolade on top of her shelve-breaking number of awards. The prestigious Granite of the year XX24 prize is discerned to the best entertainer of Deluwood and Queen V's avant-garde Western movie helps her taking the precious home. She also makes history as the first of her kind to win the Granite of the Best Western Film.

The Virgo Queen was so petrified that she almost turned to stone like a Medusa victim. Fortunately, her stylist had filled her golden corset's underwire with the antidote to ensure she could unfreeze rapidly. Queen V was moved, and her *childmager*, Yellow, encouraged her and held her hand for the speech. The Virgo Queen has spoken, "Finally, the hornets' nest is BUZZING!"

I was judgmental about this lavish ceremony – but I was mistaken. Entertainment has an undeniable healing power, and the timing couldn't be more APT! Seeing the "who's who" of "fake that" having so much fun lifts my spirit!

I love how the once adult-only event is now a lovey dovey family event. This new fusional behavior with their kids might have Deluwood's (and Power Bros') babysitters retiring sooner than expected. As long as everybody is safe and enjoys, let's ride the entertainment wave! A few years from now, I just don't want to hear any sad stories like Accordion Kids' or Brew Berrymore's.

Speaking of sad, the fortune teller Beanie Haylish, who expected to win something – like anything, must put on a smiling face as she realizes the Granites are snubbing her. I'm not a crystal gazing expert, but I think she definitely deserved a Granite hug. Luckily, her cyborg brother Nefeas is there to cover her with love and keep her afloat while she's dry drowning in her internal tears. Maybe she should let go of her signature necklace and enjoy her bright future ahead.

Speaking of bejeweled ladies, pro dancer Dobrina Esprenter's babyface blushes, as her lingerie-look swing performance is unanimously cheered by her peers. Despite that, she's ready to fire even more people than Queen V. A Legend would say, "Go do that," but she might be too focused on finding back her roaring bestie or her missing Alien fiancé, who is nowhere to be seen.

Speaking of over-the-top cheering, Mrs. Invictana is at the Granites, too. She looks stunning from head to legs, with her unlucky Ruby charm. Only *she* could have rocked a perfect X Must outfit at the Granites and served sparkling Tea! The superstar theatre diva is having fun, drinking *Copper Spade* sparkling wine, moonwalking with Victa Money's golden blazer thrown in the audience, doing the running man and the Spanky Leg to celebrate her friend The Llama's win!

The only cloud on the horizon is that she has won no Granite award this year. No teardrops on her drink, call her Mrs. Perfectly OK please – she doesn't need to do better for her alter ego's version of the *PTSD* poetry to win. She already won the most precious prize of all – Love. It's too bad Wild Valentine couldn't attend with her this year, as the NSL player has to prepare for the forthcoming grand finale with the upcoming annual Super Masked Ball.

***

Fast-forward a few days, and the pair are finally seen at the Ball, tied by the invisible string of love.

"Welcome again to your old-wild-times scene, Wild Valentine! A few years back, you were making questionable choices here in Big Easy City, and now you're back with your defending champion team, stronger than ever. How is the top dog feeling before the big poker game?" asks the interviewer.

"Thanks, I'll marry Mrs. Invictana, and it would be a pleasure to have The Phoenix as the officiant," replies the NSL player, who might suffer from an undiagnosed attention disorder.

The confused interviewer continues with questions unrelated to poker that may be banned in the future by the NSL Cut Taskforce.

"We're in Big Easy City. Have you tried the local soul food or voodoo tea?" he asks while laughing.

"I am still in my golden retriever era, but I'm dressed as The Gambler addict from Sin City. I have manifested my future wife, The Woman wearing the Sweetagette White outfit," replies the enamored but disoriented man, who is saved by another player's turn to be interviewed.

While poker players of both teams are getting ready, Sir Ron Piatiste's velvet voice shines a dusk light on the traditional Invictan hymn echoing in the stadium.

Not far from there, on the vibrant streets of Big Easy City, Lady Mama and the crowd surrounding her are showing unity and resilience where the vile act of terror was committed last month.

Then, it's time to return to the poker stadium and the actual game. The Phoenix is in attendance, and Mrs. Invictana is too, but someone gets booed – we don't know who yet.

I can't find a single reason why Mrs. Invictana would be booed, and her dumbfounded look shows we are aligned with that one. She's literally wearing a white flag while shouting, "May the best man win!" And I bet she doesn't want to add anything to her plate, as she's fragile and already dealing with the four-winged dragon allegations. Luckily, she has her family and Nice Rice by her side.

Despite that, Wild Valentine is saddened and heartbroken by the lack of manners from the supporters. Maybe what some characterize as a small, unsympathetic episode is felt by him as a murder by a hundred cuts he can only watch – helpless. The dramatics may have impacted his performance, or perhaps the third time's an unlucky Ruby charm.

I wish Mrs. Invictana could intercept my four-dimensional screams behind her library, begging her not to wear her jinx at the Ball, but to no avail.

***

There's no time for suspense.

Malone and Wild Valentine couldn't replicate their regional league's feat, and their Fountain City team lost totally. The NSL referee association couldn't even intervene, stating, "You can't have a foul play with no play."

I know that won't prevent party-boy Wild Valentine from enjoying his opponent's celebrations. Thanks to Mrs. Invictana, we all know he knows how to do that ballroom dance, and the couple is expected to stay faithful to each other in winning and losing, in loving and stalking, and in health and health.

On the other side, it's a crushing victory for their opponent from Brotherly Love City. Congratulations to the winning team's stars Sequin, Calen C., Gordan, Bilton, and Super Masked Ball's MVP Calen H.!

Brotherly Love City's mascot, Kenny Hard, is telling everyone to celebrate with *La Niña Caramina* drinks, high-pitch whistling, and barking sounds. *(Woof, Woof; Arf, Arf, Ruff, Ruff)*

I don't know the rules of this poker game, so if you have any questions about it, don't ask me, ask Goodle!

For instance, I still don't understand why some of them wear fanny packs and others don't. Maybe to collect poker chips?

***

Like many non-Invictan people, I only watch this Invictan sport once a year on Super Masked Ball Day for entertainment.

This year, there's a nice concert planned, but the most expected moment is The Llama's live cooking show.

I can't help but wonder where the other Starstrucks chefs are now. After evidently surviving a deadly bot ambush, The Dromedary finally reappears for a live cooking show at a wedding held in the crowded desert of Sunburnt Land.

As per The Dove, he's too deep in his thoughts and, just like me, has been staying home for the holidays.

Now, back to the main topic.

The Llama – now recognized as the modern days' best cook in the gourmet category – is about to start his performance at the Super Masked Ball.

Uncle Squad – the personification of Invictus Land, introduces the gig as "the great Invictan cooking game that is not just a distraction, not just a cooking show."

Then, The Llama makes his entry under a gigantic prop kitchen bell, walking confidently in the suffocating fumigated air while the erratic public cheers. He has 13 words to say to the impatient crowd: "The rebellion is broadcasted; you chose the right moment but the wrong animal."

Then he starts to cook, and the seated public progressively discovers the long-awaited menu.

The gourmet meal starter is a deconstructed poke bowl with four key ingredients (black beans, red salmon, white rice, and blueberries) displayed on a giant plate with triangle, pentagon, oval, and cross-shaped pastry cutters.

Before I have the time to scream, "It's so Octopus Game coded!" Uncle Squad comes back with the presentation of the *plat de resistance*. He now implores The Llama not to cook so-called ghetto foods like beef burgers, chitterlings, or mac and cheese.

The starred Chef feigns to please the ostentatious crowd with the chosen main meal. Everybody already knows the recipe; it's The Llama's Thankhanding's signature roast beef with even *mooooooooooooore* MUSTARD!

While pans are flying and knives are sharpened, an amateur cook passing by wants to add a decorative Maze Strip flag on the beef slice, but he's quickly expelled by security from the venue.

Then, a panicked Uncle Squad comes back to warn the public that there might be *fluffing* snakes in the *fluffing* steaks that were supposed to follow, but the astronomer Solira Luthera, who's in attendance, interjects and calms the public. Solira asks everybody to look at all the stars shining in the sky and whispers, "We are just a dot in the wider universe." After that, she promises there won't be any snakes in XX24, but she predicts an invasion of snakes and Aliens in XX25. The mysterious woman then asks the attendance: "Are You ready for hits?"

... .. .

I don't understand any of this; maybe it's another Esther egg hunt, but considering the current price of ovum, I won't participate.

This show also reminds me of Mario, and I'm not sure I'm willing to risk losing my smile. Maybe I'm projecting and *va tutto bene per Mario.*

Great, time for the 1-2 step dessert! Watermelon was banned for the event to please the stuck-up attendance, so The Llama cooks a tiramisu inspired by his recent visit to Italic Land. His apron and jeans are also a nod to Beautiful Boot Land and the illustrious Chef Pupone Tutti.

There's a brilliant twist of events right before the live cooking show ends. Sirene, a seemingly lost mermaid with new-acquired Xian legs, crashes the Super Masked Ball without a mask and starts crib walking to get to the stage to bring a gift before returning to the sea – a glass of extra virgin milk.

The Llama closes the night with twelve words:

a

Coconut

Free candies

Green light, Red light, Smile.

He Wins, Perfect.

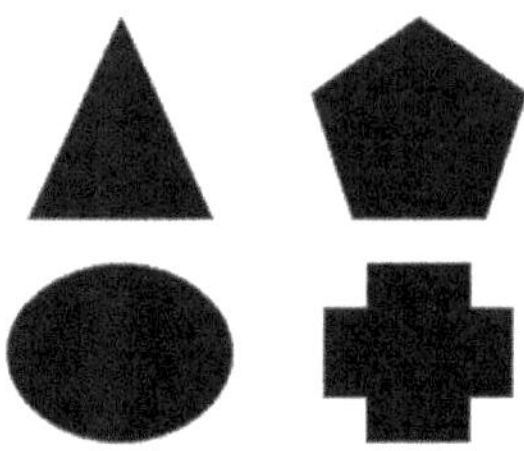

Game Over.

***

Lights Out on the Super Masked Ball.

Xieta Verse Off.

Epilogue

HELLO SILENCE, MY NEW FRIEND.

I'm sick of the noise that prevents me from hearing my thoughts and triggers panic attacks nourished by what's happening in Invictus Land while I live far away in a small, peaceful, boring town.

I'm determined to start my meditation journey, be present, and stop worrying about all these things that incapacitate me.

A wise man once said that the last month of the year is a limbo that puts every Xian at a crossroads between the past and the future.

For some, it's the only time of the year when they can be present, as if time stops to allow them to take a deep breath before resuming craziness. It resembles the quest for inner peace both Earthlings and Xians fulfill with revenge bedtime procrastination. A way to regain control of their life for a short time while their worlds sleep.

It's the perfect time to reflect on what happened, remember XX24.

Forever, XX24 will be my Novel Empire, the year I will never forget, no matter how it ends or what happens next.

I remember conspiracy theorists predicting the year XX12 to end Xians. Goodle's new quantum computer may agree that XX12 is, in fact, XX24.

I spare a thought for everyone who departed Planet X without the deserved acclaim, with a special nod to Sharon Dohany, Joe Amor, Harl Winners, Professor Violet McAbbey, Kingzy Janes, John Hurl Tones, Lili D-Town and The Best... among many others with more familiar names.

When I consider everything Xians went through this year, I can dare to say we are born resilient; it's *The Beauty of Crazy Us*.

I can't believe I made it this far, and if anyone is still reading this, I can't believe you made it this far.

I've reached the end of the last month of the longest year of all, which is making this journal thrice the size it was supposed to be.

I wanted this thirteenth month of the year of the Wool Dragon to be as sweet as my extra 14th month pay of Dreizember. Instead, my palate memory ensures I have a sour pickle flavor in my mouth. Nothing tastes the same anymore, but in all honesty, it started four years ago. XX24 was not for the faint of heart. However, this *annus horribilis* shouldn't be held responsible for it all. Events this year were just a good reminder that we're all on borrowed time. Individuality and consumerism have Xians stressed over insignificant disputes, paralyzed by things they can't control, and using escape habits that cause chronic diseases.

There's no doubt I've been doom-scrolling and binge eating.

Also, as per *Tales Magazine*, my habit of having a few drinks in a short span from time to time is called binge drinking, and it should be banned immediately. I can't believe my performative alcoholism is not the solution.

One would understand why I've avoided the body weight scale and the mirror in my bathroom this year. Today is the day to be brave enough to face up to the self-inflicted damage.

My bones creak like burdensome steps on old wooden floors, and the heaviness of time is visible on my skin.

It's time for the magic potion of Oze and snake venom injections.

I don't recognize myself and don't understand where it all went wrong. I traveled around, looking for a good scenery, but I lost myself.

I've become my own kryptonite.

***

Before I switched off the Xieta Verse, a throwback memory popped up, and I saw what I had been posting and writing 15 years before. I'm looking at a girl with a big smile who's not afraid to voice her every thought despite no one liking it or even interacting with her. I don't know if she thought no one could see her digital diary entries or if she didn't care. Her ancient blog is like a messy brain dump, sharing the many hobbies she seems to have, collecting her views on diverse topics, and unapologetically sharing her pictures. I like her, her whimsical sense of humor, and her passion for foreign languages and Lands. Multifaceted? That about sums her up.

It's funny, it's supposed to be me, but I don't recall ever being this open – about anything. If you ask me how I remember myself, I will tell you I never fit in or felt understood and was primarily undecided, full of insecurities, and scared about many things. I tried to be cool as the typical "clown class," but I've never been the badass kid who skips class. Still, despite a life with chameleon and imposture syndromes, I've never succumbed to peer pressure and always stood my ground when needed.

Education is key, as my parents have always told me not to worship Stars in the sky, never be envious of anyone, be satisfied with the little I have, keep the precious kind-hearted girl inside, and speak up when it matters. I always felt protected. Unfortunately, growing up in a fortified bird box doesn't prepare you to face the dangers of the jungle that life is. So, every stumbling block I encountered on my path made me slowly forge a metal armor to protect myself. That's how the smiley, fearless girl became the faceless sad emoji with broken wings and a dagger in her heart. Luckily, my grandmother's lessons saved me from a lot of hurt. She used to say, "Always expect to have bumps on the road; just never change your destination."

I was born a compassionate helper.

Attention, please. Empathy is a killer.

While I waste my life worrying about people who can't reciprocate the love, I kill my future and my dreams. I remember feeling for Windy Pettiams earlier this year. I bumped into her at the Golf Club the other day, doing a U-turn drift with her buggy cart and demanding to end her galaxy guardianship. I hark back to how vulnerable she was a few months ago, but she's doing better now.

Like always, people are moving on with their lives while I'm motionless. So many family members, "friends" and acquaintances are getting promoted, married, having kids, and buying houses in the suburbs, while I'm stuck in a neutral position in Camelia Street.

My parents would tell me not to compare myself to their facade and further state: "The grass is not always greener on the other side, and some of them might feel trapped in a golden cage – you never know. To each their timeline, to each their dateline."

***

Fluff it!

It's no longer my lesson to learn; I have to clear my emotional debt.

I spent my life dimming my light and blending myself into people's idea of what I should be or should do. I always brush my feelings away to not burden anyone, giving lifesaving advice I can't follow to rescue myself. Thankfully, I heartily believe that our past doesn't define our future, so it's not too late to try to either find myself back or redefine myself.

Next year, I want to make it about *me* for the first time.

I wish my new mantra to be "giving zero *fluffs*" about people's opinions and expectations. From now on, I will cut every toxicity: no gaslighting or condescending – no scrubs. Opportunely, distance and time have reduced my closed circle to fairy dust.

I imagine my future conversations:

"You're too nice, Seely."

"So what?"

"You're too weird, Seely."

"So what?"

"You're crazy, Seely."

"So what? It's YOUR turn to adapt to my newfound rebel soul."

"I'm calling you."

"Sorry, the old Seely can't talk to you right now.
Why? Because she's Red!"

Like Beckett would say, "I'm *donner* than done, giddy-up!" And I
may even want to be "*badder* than bad."

No more spending my life like Adam, giving my spot on the floating
door and sinking. We all know there's always enough place on the
buoy, but selfish people you care for would instead let you swim away
until exhaustion rather than share.

I'm not afraid anymore because I know that if I reach the coast of a
faraway island, I'll find the buried Treasured Safe, and I have the key;
no one else does. Comta Crista would rise above and heal the world
instead of taking revenge. Call me crazy now, but please continue to
call me *that* when I'll fulfill my biggest dream.

But what's that dream I keep talking about? I don't know yet; I'm
still looking for it. Maybe I should go to Golden Sparrow Land to join
a Kumbaya moment, the only Spandian event where the crowd size
can top the Allbeamings' wedding.

I should take a leap of faith and enjoy swimming in peaceful waters.
With my luck, I will end up swallowed by a whale, and I'd still laugh.
Once a black cat, always a black cat.

They say only the smartest and nicest people can laugh about
themselves. It's been established I'm nice; I'll continue to laugh until
someone believes I'm smart.

***

Even if I don't believe in Prince Charming stories, maybe deep, deep,
deep down, my vital dream is to find love.

You read that right. A research study concluded that life expectancy strongly correlates to marital status, and the winners are married. I might be reducing my life expectancy with junk food and alcohol, but at least I need to counterbalance it with sisterhood and a devotee.

All of a sudden, there's L.O.V.E in the air!

Lady Seely Clown is tired of being alone. I know love *ain't* perfect, so I shouldn't easily fall into deepfake love scams like the poor Frawnch woman who thought she was about to marry Bread Pete or the poor White Cloud Land's native who thought she had bagged the charming doctor Emerson. And I'm not mentioning the story of the gullible Grit beautician visiting North Port Land who accepted a free trip to Nueva Luna Land from a North Port Prince in exchange for fancy mules. That may be the only story with more plot holes than mine, so she's now expected to start a locked residency there.

Regardless of my desires, it would be great for happiness to find me under my rock. Maybe it's time to become Lady Love. I also want to find somebody to love, a sentimental man who will stand by me and listen to words I couldn't pronounce near my ex. Where's the space cowboy with a genuine heart that will kiss my troubles away?

May the universe give All-Time Crush the strength to find me back, see Me, and propose to invent love together. This will be an evergreen love, "dream a little dream" of Seely.

I heard from the Great Vine that All-Time Crush is prepping for a space exploration journey on a cigar-shaped vessel, so I'm realistic about the likeliness of that happening. Anyway, I'm not asking to be with the sexiest man alive – and even if I wanted to, Mr Cravinsky is taken, and I'm not Wicked. They say, "No one mourns bad girls, and no one mourns the poor." But I'd rather spend the rest of my life poor and alone than break a family or, worse, break my deep core values.

Note to self: It takes two to tango, but I will always choose a solo Sampa City dance against a passionate *paso doble* with a mischievous leprechaun.

Only one exception confirms the rule. Let me be clear: I won't try to detangle myself if I get caught in a quantum entanglement with Eyeron Peer. Who's that now? Eyeron is a corporate man who was challenged to dance by a MeTuber one day on his way to work.

The G Hugs' cheerleader team passing by hyped him up with a chant that is now viral in and out of the Xieta Verse:

"Eyeron Peer, that's my Lover!" *High Five*

"Eyeron Peer, that's my Lover!" *Turns around*

"Eyeron Peer, that's my Lover!" *Charlem shake*

"Eyeron Peer, that's my Lover!" *Head, shoulders, KNEES, and toes*

"Eyeron Peer, that's my Lover!" *Smiles while I melt.*

I never saw such a carry-on about an impromptu street performance – but hey, anything to lift spirits.

***

As the year ends, I take the time to browse my uplifting Notes-to-self journal.

Here are some extracts:

"Ill-fated life courageously lived with a childlike sparkle. Safe but cautious as a kid, scared but hopeful as a teenager, and doomed but peaceful as an adult. [...]

Being in constant fight-or-flight mode is not living; it's surviving. [...]

My journey is flawed, and that's its beauty. [...]

It's okay to have a troubled mind, but like *A* Goddess' reed, you can bend but never break. [...]

In XX24, one thing is sure, I walked through hell. [...]

Healing is remembering without hurting. [...]

I hit a record level of numbness to it all, realizing that living in the past would ruin my present and block my future. [...]

What if all this is a simulation, and my avatar only sleeps instead of trying to find the key that opens the Treasured Safe? [...]

The Stars and the galaxies are in each and every one of us. [...]

Your value is within you. If you know your worth, fight for yourself."

***

I stop right there. Didn't I pledge to ask for a promotion at some point this year?

All my enticing trips were for work purposes, aimed at bringing joy to The Xherkin's subsidiaries. Yes, I've been giving countless hours of my precious life to my corporate master during all this mess while dealing with overwhelming personal setbacks, and things couldn't be further from what I had imagined when I embarked on this career.

Thank goodness, I have a Xian Resources meeting planned soon for my Year-End Performance Review.

Oh, Dear Appraisal! You deserve an autograph – or not.

I gave it my all: explaining that my Chief Happiness Officer's salary is not aligned with my colleagues' or the market, showcasing all my outstanding achievements for the company that deserves a bigger bonus, and reminding them of my conflict resolution and team-building skills.

Drum roll

Declared, Declined, Discharged, Dismissed.

Maybe that's the haunting 4D Chess my bank account manager Tamra J. Handsome was urging me to learn. We might never know.

My stupidity overawes me. Wasted youth and unknown dreams to stay comfortably at the bottom of the corporate ladder – it's my fault. I just never tried to play the game.

No, it's my parents' fault. They taught me to play by the book and be nice, honest, and respectful. Today is the day I learned how to use an over-the-rim toilet bowl cleaner correctly, and I realized I never had the proper rules in mind. It brings to light that discreet overachievers can only win if their genius is unquestionable. I'm not a genius, so I must either amend my strategy or create my own game.

Inexistent face card, stiff-as-board dance moves, feet not marketable, too prude be my only fan, too old to find a Salt Daddy, too poor to quit, too honest to become a scammer, too scared to invest in cryptic money and my burnt-out brain doesn't seem to have a single idea. Pressed lemons can't make lemonade, so my only chance to save myself is to win the Lottery! Especially as BanKSCys keep declining my subpar loan requests for my project.

That one is my fault. After wasting my money on leisure, I can't afford to pay for the revolutionary time-traveling machine that Power Bros & Co. invented.

But I'm not completely defeated. When I looked at conspiracy boards this year, numerous hints presaged I would become a zillionaire. So, I've been pushing my luck more than ever, but I didn't want a bingo win to confirm an ironic theory, so I stopped.

Fluff it, let's try one last time!

***

On my way back from buying my last lottery ticket of XX24, I'm interrupted by a Quasar-like blinding light that almost sends my car into a ditch – a narrow escape from the sudden synchronized swerves from all vehicles on XR 375 Road. I have a kind of out-of-body experience, a sensation of levitation. Then, I see giant spermatozoid-like or snake-like meteor showers. Everybody flees, but I'm not scared for the first time in my life, and I wait in the middle of the road.

I don't know how long I stay there until I notice UFOs (or drones?) hovering above my head. I can't describe the vessels, but I feel Their presence. I feel… Them. Maybe Willi Winkatt's prophecy is happening before my eyes. It can only be Them, Aliens that had invaded The Dandy's house. Are they coming to get us, warn us of an incoming threat, or help us with the long-awaited reveal of the infamous List? Maybe this is for the greater good, as an external common enemy might be the only solution for all Xians to come together and stop fighting for dirt.

It's funny to think that if I decide to explore further planets, I'd be called an Alien. I'm just a Xian, not a threat. Who in the universe could be afraid of little old Seely? If only I had enough friends, I would take 100 of them for my YONO's arch to explore the universe. All the more so, as I learned, there's a 3.1% chance that Asteroid XX24 ZR4 will hit Planet X in year XX32, right after the end of my 7-year project.

When two worlds collide, you must brace for impact – but Xians don't look up; they concentrate on hunger games.

Incredible! I can't believe I'm dissociating in the middle of an Alien invasion. I'm wondering if that's what happened in Sampa City when a woman kept her composure while held hostage by a demented captor at the train station on her way to work. She's me, I'm her, like, "Get it over with already!"

Life can flip in one second. We're always on the verge of a close shave and a new normal without acknowledging it.

What if it's the end? How would I be remembered? Did I leave my footprints on Planet X?

That's when I get an interstellar slap in the face, and I hear those words:

"Deadass serious...

The intergalactic portal will be opened at Treasure Beach for 13 days, a fortnight, or... MORE!

It's your chance to connect with otherworldly beings and spread love.

Leave nothing unsaid; save your story, Xian history, and Planet X memory.

On Moon C New Year, drop your time capsule at the foot of the lighthouse and mark the timestamp on the sand. One copy will be preserved in the safest place here, and the other will be sent to the planet of your choice. Be careful; only authentic and organic materials are allowed if an atmospheric entry is expected.

Be reassured: if your material is considered too damaged and/or uninterpretable, we'll facilitate a clean version for the host planet.

Beware of keeping a safe distance around midnight, or you'll get lured into the wormhole.

Now, wake up, shut up and write."

A split second later, there's no one around, and the presence I felt is gone. I know no one will ever believe me. But they were there, they were fair – I remember them all too jelled.

No, I don't – but my Alien encounter is real; I swear!

Still astounded, I hit the floor and went for a ride to clear my mind. When I stop at a red light, I recall what I used to do with my aunt Karina when I was a kid, blowing on red traffic lights to turn them green. For the first time in my life, it works on the first try! I'm so excited I jump hysterically behind the wheel. I must look like a fool as the driver next to me stares at me bewilderedly. Guess what? I'm giving zero *fluffs*! I look at my watch: 13:13. It must be a sign from the universe that my luck is coming, and I should believe in myself!

I need to put my life in order first. When I get back home, I tidy up my hoarded house. I find so many things I've been looking for – hidden in unsuspected places. I even find back the 13-printed merch tote bag from *The Auras*. While cleaning, I remember Ellie explaining the meaning behind the number 13. Again, what would my life be like if I had tried to follow my dream when I was 13? What if I had felt like I could be unapologetically crazy-me with my crazy fantasies without fearing being judged or scolded?

It's now as limpid as Triangulum Islands' waters.

Open your eyes, Seely.... Open your eyes.. Open your eyes.

***

Dolly Zoom effect...

Aha moment..

Hourglass.

Hourglass.

Aha moment..

Dolly Zoom effect...

***

This is my time capsule, destined for Planet Earth.

Known for its mesmerizing Blue and beautiful Earthlings as Blue as Flurfs, the choice was easy.

I figured this ancient form of writing would be more suitable for the least developed beings of the Solar System. The only issue is that I know nothing about writing or character development...

I only have 13 days or a fortnight to draw the perfect plot diagram before the intergalactic portal closes, and I'm choking on too big of a word salad to swallow. Writing is a titanic task.

I feel invisible; it's horrible, and nobody knows!

I can't make it happen, no way! But I like the idea; it's fun!

At least, it felt like it until I realized it's more complicated than I thought to find the right words to convey what I bear in mind and what I harbor in my Xian heart. Trying to write after an exhausting workday, procrastinating during the weekend, getting sick, doubting, giving up, pushing through, giving up again, finding encouragement from strangers, giving it a try slowly, word by word... starting without knowing where it would land and if it will end up full-circling.

In the meantime, here I am... still writing.

Wait! Is that an unwanted digital brain that jumped into my organic time capsule?

Mind you, I happily followed a material and digital minimalism during this process, avoiding GP Transformer robot, The Cat and others.

I'm so disappointed by The Gatekeeper! Some people might tell me it was expected with the impending tidal wave of Dip Script and the urge to find other ways to innovate. If you ask me, doing it at the expense of users is not the best solution. Where's consent and the switch-off button in all that? If even Exron can't deal with that mess, imagine how a nobody would feel about it!

I want to quit now. It's there, everywhere – Autopilot, following my every step and every word. What if it offers a clone of my time capsule to a lazy Xian with writer's block?

I must be dumb; I can't get rid of it! But it's my fault again – if I hadn't procrastinated, I wouldn't have been in this situation, and it wouldn't have a dedicated paragraph.

If you ask, I don't care about being called fragile or Soft for being pressed about Autopilot stalking me. I want to quit so bad, but I put my mental health at risk for this, and I'll be stuck forever in a bootstrap paradox if I don't send it to the universe.

I've seen Big K warriors and everyday soldiers fighting the hardest battles – so I'm pushing through despite the colored square nightmare.

My atelophobia made me quit several times, but my mystical pronoia is stronger than ever.

I'm doing it sober, adjusting my archer to hit my goal of connecting Earthlings together. The word on the universe is that they're stuck in a nonsensical quarrel loop and are entering a loneliness epidemic.

If it weren't my dream to write this text, maybe it could be theirs to read.

Now I can tell You that this is the story of a dream chaser who caught something special in her nets, the biggest dream that ever lived. Gabe Churchelle would be proud of me – but he won't have the chance to read it. If this time capsule doesn't wind up gathering nebular dust, the lucky ones who may read it are beautiful Earthlings.

I don't expect anyone to understand it alone; it would be a collective effort to assemble the puzzle of XX24 and find the Treasured Safe somewhere... or nowhere.

If my time capsule gets discovered by chance or by Goodle's grace in *The Jungle*, it might change Earthlings' destiny forever... or not.

Let's hope it won't be a thunderclap making underwater cables snap and causing a blackout on Planet Earth.

***

Maybe

Maybe my signal will be a white noise sent to the intergalactic void.
Maybe I should take more time and risk passing my expiry date.
Maybe I shouldn't use a self-diagnosis to explain my lack of attention span and motivation.
Maybe judgy Judys and Rudys will concentrate on irrelevant issues and apparent mistakes, thus overlooking the positive message.
Maybe nice Nancys will devote heart and soul to defending me and my intentions.
Maybe Not.
Maybe one day, I'll be able to ban crutch words, adverbs, "maybes," "buts," dots, parentheses, and ellipses...
Maybe I should show, not tell.
Maybe I don't want to.
Maybe I should start my time capsule with a disclaimer...

***

I'm sick to my stomach, with joy stuck in my throat – it's done.

It felt good to bare my soul, but the more I think about it, the more terrified I am of anyone reading this.

After risking my sanity, I have no choice but to send it tonight to the portal, hoping it will reach the celestial orb of my dreams.

As instructed by the Alien presence, I go to Treasure Beach, I put down my time capsule at the bottom of the lighthouse, I write XX24 in the sand, and leave.

***

Staying home for New Year's Eve allows me to reflect on my abandoned dreams about to cruise the universe like ancient lanterns floating in the air and dancing in the sky.

Sitting on my front porch with my red cardigan, alone in the cold, dark night, I'm ready to treat my body like a temple.

I'm starting my ultimate attempt at a dry January with 13 round fruits, a good old hot chocolate, and a turnip cake.

I'm looking at the stars, committed to appreciating what I have, cherishing time spent with the people I love, and stop running away.

***

Let's all relax and SMILE.

Let's create our space and return to our roots: simple pleasures, conversations, bonds, love, and fun.

I can't believe I abandoned one of my sweetest forms of escape.

Let's find other getaways next year; let's find ourselves a good melody.

***

We leave the year of the Wool Dragon to enter the year of the Wool
Snake.

Here's to health, stealth, wealth, and elves!

I wish You luck in your dreams, love in your heart, and peace in your
mind for XX25.

May the next 14 months be filled with joy.

Happy New Year!

***

Pardon me; I lost my train of thought again.
I forgot to say I fulfilled one of my delusional promises.
I wrote a song.
I don't remember when I did, but I found it in the bin while cleaning
out my closet – a crumpled paper ball titled
"Clover River."

***

Clover River

A bird nest felt from the tree
The wind picked it up and put it to rest
By the right bank of Treasure Beach
Giving it a chance to fledge with its crest

A hunter found a good scenery
But she lost sight of her story to tell
By the left bank of Treasure Beach
Words fading on her ode to belles

Oh oh
Oh oh oh
Sealing her fate to be a caged bird singing
Oh oh
Oh oh oh
Forgetting she's everything she thinks she's not
Oh oh
Oh oh
Oh oh oh
Screeching noise of a broken-hearted sword

A wise man whispered on her ear
Live for the cause, don't perish for it
It echoed, like stones skipping
On the shiny surface of Clover River

A dreamer got down on her knees
Apologizing for missing the beat
The rain kissed her eyes then her cheeks
She ran away, leaving her dreams

Oh oh
Oh oh oh
Sealing her fate to be a caged bird singing
Oh oh
Oh oh oh
Forgetting she's everything she thinks she's not
Oh oh
Oh oh
Oh oh oh
Screeching noise of a broken-hearted sword

That erased everything step she took
Cut every bond she made
Ripped every hope she had
Oh oh oh
She numbed all her pain with grace
Armored her heart with chains
Locked in a Treasured Safe

...

Whose key has been thrown
Away

..

That may be found

.

One day

(musical bridge)

A fisher
Caught a prize in her nets
When visiting her old town
In the center of the river
Deep
She remembered
It
Was
Hers

Oh oh

Oh oh oh

Her precious secrets wrapped up in her chest

Singing

Oh oh

Oh oh oh

The Treasured Safe You've been looking for

***

Let's include that in my time capsule!
I hope it's not too late.
I'm going back to Treasure Beach.
Fingers crossed, wish me luck.

***

***

Is that a wormhole or a black hole?

***

www.ingramcontent.com/pod-product-compliance
Lightning Source LLC
Chambersburg PA
CBHW050320160726
48002CB00001B/116